Cat and Mouse
A Lesbian Romance Spanking Novella

Cat and Mouse
A Lesbian Romance Spanking Novella

By Clarine Klein

http://clarineklein.com

Cassidy Coleman is a sassy, but rather introverted college sophomore out on her own for the first time ever in her young adult life. At the start of fall semester, she moves into an apartment along with a randomly assigned roommate from her university, Lauren Delaney. Lauren is a an outgoing and athletic economics major one year ahead of Cassidy in school, and is just looking for a place to live that doesn't also double up as a party house on the weekends.

And from day one, Cassidy is smitten.

Unfortunately for her though, things are more than a little awkward between the two of them for the first several weeks of the new semester, with Cassidy too tongue-tied to properly carry on more than a two sentence conversation before needing to flee to her bedroom. Eventually though, the two bond over a mutual love of video games from their childhood one evening, and overnight an instant and lifelong friendship is forged.

From there friendship soon blossoms into love, but with a twist.

Cassidy is a total brat and loves nothing more than to find excuses to push her long-suffering roommate's buttons. Not too long after their friendship is formed, they fall into a routine of Cassidy seeing how far she can push things before Lauren finally snaps and scolds her. It's a fun game of cat and mouse that they both enjoy, but one day things take a step further when Cassidy ends up pushing her best friend into a freezing pool on a chilly winter night! Laughing uproariously at her sputtering roommate, she suddenly finds herself being draped across her lap for a well-earned spanking.

That spanking ends up throwing open the doors on advancing their relationship, out of the sexually tense stalemate they'd found themselves in, and after having her bottom thoroughly reddened, Cassidy all but pounces on her roommate and best friend right there and then, kissing her for all she's worth. From there, things only get steamier as the two of them start to fall more and more in love with each other and in the process explore their mutual love language.

Spanking and discipline.

Chapter 1

"You think I won't?"

College sophomore Cassidy Coleman's stomach was abuzz with nervous excitement as she huffed and puffed her way up the two flights of pitted cement stairs that led to her brand new on-campus apartment. Wobbling a bit on unsteady feet, she attempted to negotiate her way around the as yet unfamiliar layout of her living room while her hands slipped and scrabbled desperately to cling to the bulging sides of the cardboard box stuffed near to bursting that was obscuring most of her view. Reaching her bedroom, or at least what she hoped was her bedroom, she gave an almighty shove to force the stubborn box through the narrow gap of the doorframe, and stumbled forward. She managed to make it across the threshold of the tiny room just as the box tumbled out of her hands to land with a heavy "thwump" at the foot of her bed, one of its sides splitting open and disgorging its contents across the faded carpet all around it.

"Eh, close enough," she shrugged.

Heaving out an exhausted sigh and not caring at all where the wrinkled pile of panties, tops, and skirts landed, so long as it was somewhere within the general confines of her bedroom, Cassidy stumbled over the ruined mound of cardboard and flopped face first onto her bare mattress, bouncing lightly with the impact and smiling to herself as she did her best to try and get a grip on the butterflies scrambling around inside her stomach.

On the one hand she was ecstatic to finally be officially out on her own. Living with her parents had been okay enough at first after she'd graduated from high school, she'd paid them rent and they'd said she was free to come and go as she pleased while living with them, but it just wasn't the same as *really* being independent in her eyes. Now she had her very own apartment to call her own, a place where she'd never have to worry about getting sidelong glances from her mother whenever she asked her how late she'd stayed up the night before, or have to put up with her father bursting into her bedroom at noon to fling back her covers and "suggest" she get out of bed. To say nothing of the way her parents seemed to routinely forget that she was a woman in her early twenties, not some bratty tween who needed a firm pat on the seat to get her moving whenever there were chores to be done. Nope, she was finally her own boss, living all by herself in a tiny on-campus apartment that was all her own.

Well, *mostly* all her own. The problem with moving out of her parents' house as a basically penniless college student was that Cassidy couldn't exactly afford to foot the bill for an apartment all by herself, which meant she either had to make herself beholden to her parents by letting them cover her rent, which was the last thing she felt like doing, or she needed to find some roommates. Unfortunately for her, all of her friends from high school, community college, and the few months she'd worked at the local movie theater by her parents' house during the summer were either married and getting ready to pop out kids of their own, or were off at different schools out of state, which left her with no other choice than to throw herself on the mercy of the random roommate assignment program her school offered and hope for the best.

And that's where Lauren Delaney came into the picture. She was an economics major one year ahead of Cassidy at their university who'd had a less than stellar time last semester splitting the rent on a dilapidated party house just off the edge of campus with a few of the friends she'd met freshman year. After one sleepless night trying to study while her other roommates blasted music as loud as they could too many, she'd finally gotten fed up with her situation and decided to try her luck with the roommate lottery for the fall semester so she could *actually* focus on her program and not have to live in an overcrowded house that constantly reeked of stale beer and moldy pizza. And so far, she had to admit to herself as she finished breaking down the last cardboard box of her stuff and stashed it away in the back of her bedroom closet in the cozy little apartment she'd been assigned, things were already starting to look up. Her new place was clean, especially compared to the pig sty she'd just come from, it was way closer to campus, it had nice thick walls that kept the noise from their next door neighbors to a minimum, and best of all it even came with a single adorable roommate.

From the moment the older girl had first introduced herself to her, Cassidy had been smitten. Lauren Delaney was easily half a foot taller than she was (which wasn't really saying all that much given her diminutive five foot, one inch frame), with well-toned shoulders and arms, and a firm handshake that reminded Cassidy of one of her high school volleyball coaches and made her stomach flutter in a not-unpleasant way for some reason. Despite her rather impressive and somewhat imposing physique, it was the way Lauren carried herself that *really* drew in Cassidy like a moth to a flame. She had a strong, angular face with rich, full lips that always seemed to be bent upward into a perpetual half-smirk, like she'd just remembered the punch line to a joke she'd heard the night before. Her voice had a casual lilt to it as if she knew exactly what you were thinking whenever she spoke with you, and a wry sense of humor to go with it. And when she moved, it was with a natural and understated athletic grace that made Cassidy feel gangly and uncoordinated by comparison. In her eyes, Lauren Delaney was easily the most impressive and captivating person she'd ever met, and Cassidy had no idea how to handle that.

For the first few weeks after moving in, Cassidy and Lauren mostly just kept to themselves. Between the hectic start of a new semester and the usual awkward speed bumps of getting to know someone new and settling into a new home in unfamiliar surroundings, they usually only saw each other in passing, and when they did they usually exchanged little more than a casual "hello" or "did you have a good day?" before moving off to the privacy of their own bedrooms. Lauren for her part just assumed that her new roommate wasn't the talkative sort, or that maybe she didn't like her for some reason, whereas Cassidy very much liked her new roommate, but was way too intimidated to strike up more than a casual conversation with her lest she look like an idiot. There was just something about the older girl that set Cassidy's heart fluttering and her stomach flip-flopping whenever she was around her, leaving her tongue tied and feeling like she had to do something, *anything*, to fill the awkward silence that seemed to bubble up between the two of them whenever they were in the same room. But rather than risk humiliating herself by doing or saying something stupid, Cassidy would routinely clam up after only a few half-hearted attempts at a conversation and then make up an excuse to rush off and hide in her room, promising herself that she'd try again some other time and that things would be different then.

The two of them continued on in their increasingly uncomfortably-tense status-quo for several long weeks until one fateful evening during Thanksgiving break when things suddenly changed. Cassidy had just returned home to their apartment after spending the day with her parents and extended family, gorging on turkey, mashed potatoes, and way too many types of pie, and she'd brought back with her a few more boxes of stuff that she hadn't had room for in her car when she'd first moved in. Specifically, her Super Nintendo and the not-insubstantial library of games she'd managed to build up for it over the years since she was a child.

"Whoa, is that a Nintendo?"

The question startled Cassidy, making her jerk in surprise and bump the back of her head against the painted cinderblock wall behind her while she remained bent over half-stuck and half-wedged behind their small TV in their living room, balancing with one foot in the air and trying to feel out where she could plug her game console into. She'd been so excited to get her system set up that she hadn't even realized Lauren was home, and hadn't heard her come out of her bedroom either. How long had she been standing there watching her for? Oh god, she must look like such a doofus!

"Oh! Um, yeah it is," she confirmed with a sudden flush of heat in her cheeks, blowing several strands of honey blonde hair out of her face and attempting to reach back with her free hand to try and smooth down the back of her short denim skirt where she could feel it riding up to show off the dancing turkeys stretched tautly across the seat of her panties. Several finger-fumbling moments later she finally managed to slip the ends of the game console's AV cables into what were probably the correct spots on the back of the rickety, old TV, and with a sigh of relief and another puff of air to try and stop her hair from tickling her nose, she awkwardly levered herself out from behind their cinderblock and plywood media center.

"Awesome, I haven't seen one of those in years."

Lauren's sharp eyes had indeed not missed the sight of the adorable turkeys cavorting across the back of her roommate's panties, nor had she failed to notice just how cute of a caboose Cassidy had as she inadvertently waggled it back and forth at her while she fished her arm behind their TV. Part of her was sorely tempted to move in closer and help her roommate "stay balanced" by grabbing a handful of what was surely an exquisitely squishable set of cheeks, but she resisted that urge and instead settled down onto their threadbare, faux-suede sofa and turned her attention to running her fingertips along the gray plastic tops of the game cartridges stacked in neatly-packed rows in the cardboard box beside her.

"Oh hey, Super Mario World!" Lauren's eyes lit up with excitement as she deftly plucked the game in question from between the others and gave its front a perfunctory dusting with the sleeve of her sweater. "My friends and I used to play this one all the time when we were kids."

Cassidy, who loved her childhood video games dearly, was more than a little surprised to find her roommate showing so much interest in them. Even though Lauren was only a year older than her, in her mind's eye Cassidy had somehow always pictured her as just being a tiny and just as mysterious version of who she was now when she was younger. It hadn't occurred to her that Lauren was probably just like any other person when she was growing up, spending her afternoons after school at friends' houses playing games and messing around getting into trouble.

"You want to play?" she asked tentatively, trying to sound casual and hoping against hope that her roommate's seeming interest wasn't actually just more idle small talk. "I've got two controllers."

"Sure, sounds like fun," agreed Lauren with a flip of her hair, passing the cartridge off to her roommate and settling back onto the couch with an eager expression to watch as Cassidy knelt down and slotted the game into the top of her Super Nintendo and then fished out two of the controllers from her box of wires and various other accessories.

And just like that, the two of them settled in for what would end up being an all-night session of nostalgic retro gaming. Huddling together on the couch for warmth against the late fall chill seeping in through their drafty windows, they battled their way through level after level, stopping only to gorge themselves on Pizza Hut in their pajamas when they eventually got hungry, and getting to know one another on a deeply personal level in between frantic and excited cries of "Oh, oh! Right there, jump!" and "Darn it! That was so close!" When the sun had finally risen the following morning, its warm rays pouring into their living room through slotted blinds only half-drawn, it found the two of them dozed off and cuddled up together on the couch beneath a thick blanket Lauren had brought out from her room. Without even realizing it had happened, Cassidy and Lauren had stumbled onto a bit of common ground that had managed to obliterate the weeks of awkward tension that had been building between the two of them in a single night, sweeping it aside and replacing it with an instant connection and a fondness that would only grow stronger as time went on.

—

After that fateful Thanksgiving night, Cassidy and Lauren had become fast friends, and by the time Christmas break had come and gone, the two of them were practically inseparable. School kept the two of them busy most nights and weekends, but even when one of them was caught up in research or homework, the other typically wasn't too far behind, content-ing themselves with idling away their time on something of their own in the same room while the other worked, simply enjoying being in each other's company even if they weren't "doing" anything together. Lauren still carried herself with the same understated grace and confident half-smirk that made Cassidy's stomach flutter whenever she daydreamed about her when she was alone, but rather than be intimidated by her roommate as she had been for so long, Lauren's demeanor now just made Cassidy smile fondly to herself. Well, usually. Ever since their impromptu slumber party, Lauren had come to understand just how it was she made her bubbly roommate feel, and how easily she could make her squirm and blush the most adorable shade of scarlet whenever she felt like it; which was something she rarely missed the opportunity to take advantage of.

All she had to do was point at a pile of dirty dishes in the sink Cassidy hadn't gotten around to scrubbing yet, or raise an eyebrow at the mound of laundry she might have left sitting in their dryer for several days in a row, and Cassidy's heart would skip a beat, the pit of her stomach would do several flip flops, and she'd find her mouth had gone suddenly dry like she'd just stepped into the lair of a hungry predator who planned on toying with her before moving in for the kill. Not that she minded. Those moments of friendly sharpness always left Cassidy's knees wonderfully wobbly and gripped her lower abdomen with a heady tightness that could last all evening. A look or a point was all it would take, and then Cassidy would spring into action, squeak out an embarrassed excuse, and then scramble to take care of whatever it was she'd left undone while her roommate watched on with a wider smirk than usual. Lauren in turn would just laugh to herself in that sultry way of hers, maybe waggle an admonishing finger at her friend and tell her not to let it happen again, and that would be that. At least until the next time.

Opportunities for these lighthearted scolding sessions seemed to present themselves about once every other day, and sometimes twice in the same day on rare occasions. Without either of them even realizing it had happened, the two of them had spun it off into a little game. Cassidy would look for ways to try her friend's patience or get a rise out of her, most of the time on purpose but more often than not it seemed she just had a natural talent for inadvertently pushing the older girl's buttons, and Lauren would pounce, smirking in mock-disapproval and playfully lecturing her friend whenever she "caught" her being a brat. It was a simple game of cat and mouse, and one they both enjoyed thoroughly, though neither of them could pinpoint just when it was they'd started playing it.

Little did they realize that in just a few short weeks, on

a cold winter night neither of them would ever forget, their game would take on an entirely new dimension.

It was nearing the end of February, and the frigid grip of the icy winds that had been holding the grounds of Cassidy and Lauren's college campus hostage for the last few weeks was finally starting to ease up as the sun started to shine more and more each day. Even better, the two of them had just finished their last midterms for the semester that afternoon and they had a three day weekend ahead of them to look forward to. To celebrate, Cassidy had managed to talk her roommate into "breaking into" her aunt and uncle's house so that they could use their hot tub while they were away on vacation. Truth be told, her relatives had actually given her a spare key to their house so she could pop in every week or so to check the mail and look after the place while they were gone, and while they hadn't *actually* given her permission to make use of their rather impressive (and very expensive) outdoor kitchen and swimming pool setup, Cassidy was pretty sure that they wouldn't mind so long as she and Lauren cleaned up after themselves.

Well, probably.

Either way it was much more fun to pretend that the whole thing was some sort of clandestine adventure they had to stealth their way through, rather than just taking advantage of her extended family's hospitality. In any case, other than flashing her best friend a dubious look when she'd reassured her a little too quickly that her aunt and uncle wouldn't mind them coming over, really, honestly, they totally wouldn't, Lauren had agreed. And so later that night the two of them slipped through the big house's back door under the cover of darkness, save for the myriad strings of hanging bulb-lights strewn all around the deck that Cassidy had flipped on while raiding her aunt and uncle's refrigerator for a few hard ciders, giddily anticipating the chance to spoil themselves for a couple of hours.

Shivering as the occasional chilly gust stirred up around them and complaining animatedly about how cold the paving stones felt beneath their bare feet, they stripped off their lightweight exercise shorts and zip-up hoodies and all but sprinted for the steamy embrace of the luxury Jacuzzi that was the crown jewel of Cassidy's uncle's backyard oasis. The two of them laughed and gasped with the shock of the sudden shift in temperature as they sat down along its contoured edge and slipped their feet into the foamy, frothing water right in front of them, easing themselves forward until the bubbles lapped happily at them from just below their knees. The contrast in temperature between the hot tub and the crisp night air felt absolutely wonderful, and with long sighs and the occasional groan of pleasure, Lauren and Cassidy wriggled their bikini-clad butts further forward, until with a sudden splash, they were submerged beneath the water, settling down onto the stone bench under the roiling surface with a soft "thump". Neither of them said much of anything for several long minutes, instead just basking in the gently insistent massage of the air jets blowing firm streams of bubbles against their backs, gradually easing away the tension in their tired muscles as their eyes studied the backs of their eyelids and their thoughts drifted away across the surface of the bubbling cauldron they sat in.

"Oh my god, this is the *best*," moaned Lauren, twisting in her seat to reach back behind her and pop the caps off of a pair of hard apple ciders.

"No, kidding," nodded Cassidy, drawing the words out with a mellow sigh before taking a long pull from the bottle her friend had just passed her. "I love soaking in a hot tub when it's all chilly like this. The cold air and the hot water mixing together makes it all feel so *magical*."

She made a broad, sweeping gesture with her bottle, taking in the rising columns of steam coiling up all around them as they sat nice and warm amid the patchy blanket of hard-packed snow still covering some areas of the grass along the outer edges of the back yard, accidentally splashing more than a little bit of her drink onto her friend's shoulder with the motion.

"Hey, watch it!" protested Lauren, wiping away the sticky cider from her shoulder with her free hand before sinking lower into the water to let the tub rinse away what was left. There was no heat in her voice however, and she and Cassidy just laughed it off as they eased back into another companionable silence.

After a while though they started to get bored of just sitting around stewing in their own private thoughts, and with a small splash from Cassidy that earned her a satisfyingly annoyed look from her best friend, their conversation picked up again. For the better part of the next forty-five minutes the two of them laughed and gossiped their way through chatting about how they'd done on their respective midterms, ideas for things to do during their upcoming spring break, stories of the time Cassidy and her cousin had thrown a huge party in this very back yard while her aunt and uncle had supposedly been away on a night out, and a handful of random other things that just so happened to come up as their conversation meandered from one topic to the next.

As they soaked, their bodies gradually grew accustomed to the heat of the tub, and to counter this they would periodically push themselves back up to sit on the stone edge by the water, letting the frosty night air chill them all over again before slipping back into the hot water's embrace as if they'd never left. It was during one of these re-acclimating periods, that it happened. Lauren had been standing near the edge of the large swimming pool, admiring its dark, rippling surface in the warm glow of the bulb-lights as she stretched her arms over her head and yawned, when without warning, Cassidy sprang into action behind her.

"Surprise!" she cried, shoving her friend from behind and catching her completely off-guard, sending her stumbling forward and into the pool with a mighty splash that managed to soak the paving stones she'd just been standing on.

Lauren surfaced a moment later, spluttering and gasping in counterpoint to Cassidy's side-splitting laughter from where she stood only a few feet away from her, hugging herself and wiping away a tear from her eye. With a low growl, Lauren flew toward the edge of the pool just as fast as her freezing limbs would allow, her strong arms and legs making short work of the wintry water before levering herself up and out back onto the cement just a few feet from her traitorous roommate.

"Y-You little brat!" she gasped around trembling lips, fuming with indignation while also starting to laugh despite herself. Cassidy always seemed to have that effect on her.

"What was that?" taunted Cassidy, leaning forward with a self-satisfied smirk plastered across her face and one hand cupped around an ear. "I couldn't hear you over all that shivering."

"Why you," growled Lauren, still grinning as she pushed back her sopping wet hair from her narrowed eyes and straightened up to her full height. Spurred on by the sudden burst of adrenaline still coursing through her veins, her initial indignation had rapidly melted away to be replaced by a sudden and devious plan as an idle daydream that had bouncing around in the back of her mind for weeks now suddenly snapped into focus. "I ought to put you over my knee right here and now for that little stunt!"

Those words hit Cassidy like a lightning bolt, cutting her laughter short as the familiar wobbly knees and flood of heat in her lower abdomen suddenly gripped her tighter than ever, rooting her to the spot where she stood as a full-body flush signaled just what she thought about *that* particular idea. Part of her knew she could just laugh the whole thing off as a joke, ignore her roommate's threat and slip back into the hot tub like nothing had ever happened, and that would be the end of it. But instead she found herself taking a tentative step back and whining. "Oh come on, Lauren, it was just a joke! You can't be serious."

She hoped to god she was though.

Sensing she'd struck a nerve, Lauren's usual half-smirk widened into a full on grin as she took one confident step forward and then another, cocking an eyebrow and fixing her friend with her best intimidating stare.

"You think I won't?"

Cassidy swallowed hard at that, sensing that things were suddenly moving very fast in a direction that up until just a moment ago had been exclusively the stuff of her nighttime fantasies as she lay curled up under her sheets with her magic wand. Her mouth had gone dry, and as her roommate and best friend advanced on her, she understood that Lauren was waiting for her to give her the go ahead. Without it needing to be said, she knew that this was her last chance to back out, to say "Nope, I'm fine, thanks!" and move on. Resisting that urge however, she instead decided to throw caution to the wind and see what would happen next. And so, putting as much sass and contempt as she could muster into her voice, she spat out her reply with a challenging grin of her own.

"I'd like to see you try."

Rather than say anything, Lauren just barked out an amused laugh at that, and far quicker than Cassidy had been expecting, closed the distance between the two of them and snatched up her wrist in an iron grip. Moving without a moment's hesitation, she dragged her now frantically protesting best friend over to the nearest poolside lounger she could find, settling down onto its webbed seat with a graceful plop, before yanking Cassidy across her lap with casual ease. The girl landed with a heavy "oomph!" across Lauren's strong thighs, her warm weight settling pleasantly across her lap with her adorable bubble-butt perched perfectly to offer up its generous curves, practically *begging* to be spanked as a fresh round of half-hearted whining started up once again from its owner, going totally ignored.

Cassidy's nervous stream of babbling excuses and attempts to stall quickly devolved into a series of disconnected squeaks and yelps as Lauren wasted no time in starting to pepper her still-wet backside with hard, full-strength, open-palmed slaps aimed at the meatiest parts of each cheek and the delicate undercurves peeking out just below her white bikini. She watched with mounting excitement and more than a little hunger as her best friend's ample hips began to squirm and wriggle in a mesmerizing pattern, bouncing and wobbling as they flattened and sprang back for more under the relentless fury of her right palm. Lauren didn't bother with lecturing her friend while she worked, they both knew she wasn't *actually* mad at her for pushing her into the pool, and instead focused her efforts on spreading as much sharp heat and relentless sting as she could across Cassidy's rapidly shifting bottom, pouring all of her considerable strength into each swat, spurred on by the ever increasing yelps of surprise and squeals of pain that were her reward with each new spank. It was an intoxicating experience, more exhilarating than even beating Cassidy at Mario Kart, and Lauren found that she couldn't get enough.

After an initial blitz of some thirty or forty world-class spanks, Lauren took a moment to let her palm rest against the back of Cassidy's swimsuit, drinking in the warmth radiating up from beneath the damp material as her best friend lay across her lap, panting. She watched on with wry amusement as Cassidy tried to catch her breath, feeling her cheeks shifting with each exhalation as her twin orbs clenched and unclenched beneath the thin layer of taut nylon that had been their only protection as they'd reddened under Lauren's efforts. Though for now her cheeks only showed the faintest hint of pink beneath the uniform white material clinging to them like a second skin, more vivid traces of color could be seen peeking out from where her swimsuit had ridden up between them, and the sight of it made Lauren's mouth water as she tried to imagine just how red she could make her best friend's bottom be before she'd had enough. After a few more moments of casual groping and rubbing, she decided that she'd given her errant roommate enough of a break, she didn't want her to think she was getting off lightly after all, and with a predatory grin stretched wide across her lips, she slipped her fingers into the stretchy waistband of the bikini bottoms in front of her.

"I've been dying for a chance to get my hands on this adorable little ass of yours for a while now, so thanks for the opportunity," she teased, pulling her waistband up and back to expose the very tops of Cassidy's cheeks, her grin widening even more as she watched them break out in goose bumps.

Cassidy for her part sputtered out an incomprehensible squawk of indignation as her face flushed nearly as hot as her bottom felt. She started to squirm again, though not very hard in case her wriggling inadvertently worked her swimsuit even further down her hips, when it suddenly dawned on her just *where* it was they were just then. Humiliating visions of her aunt and uncle's neighbors poking a head out their windows or leaning over fences to see what all the noise was about suddenly danced across her mind's eye, setting off a fresh round of butterflies in her lower abdomen as her thighs moved on autopilot to squeeze and rub together. With a squeak, she clamped her two fists tight over her mouth, sucking on her knuckles and moaning with impotent frustration as the utter humiliation of it all washed over her, loving every second of it despite herself.

"That's right," cooed Lauren, her voice carrying a cruel smile as she ever so slowly peeled away Cassidy's clinging swimsuit an inch at a time until she'd exposed the whole of her best friend's silky smooth buttocks to the chilly night air around them, along with any unseen watchers her nerve-addled imagination might have conjured up. She then compounded her embarrassment tenfold with a sharp tug that snapped the wet garment down her thighs where it came to a sudden stop, bunching loosely around her slightly bent knees, still dripping. "You just hush and take your medicine like a good girl. Okay, cutie pie?"

"Eep! Yes ma'am!"

Cassidy felt a low chuckle reverberate through her side from where she lay snuggled up against her best friend's surprisingly strong midriff, which in turn coaxed out even more whining from her as she scissored her ankles back and forth with a pout. Her heart was racing now and she gasped at the feel of Lauren's comparatively cold hands as they sought out every curve of the skin they'd just exposed, heedless of her moaning as they quested and probed, squeezed and parted her now bare cheeks; testing their elasticity and admiring what lay hidden between them, before suddenly unleashing an avalanche of spanks that sent her reeling.

Without a swimsuit to hold it in place, Cassidy's bottom bounced and wobbled freely with each and every smack of Lauren's palm, rippling with the force of its impact before immediately springing back for more as if it'd been made for just such a purpose all along. A fact that did not go unnoticed by either of them as they each tucked it away for later reflection when they were alone again in their respective beds. Lauren was relentless, encouraged ever onward to swat harder and faster by Cassidy's hissed squeals of pain through gritted teeth in between her murmured cries of "Holy cow!" and "Owieowieowie!". She squirmed ineffectually in the steel vice that was her best friend's left arm wrapped firmly around her waist, pinning her in place as she flailed her legs to and fro as if she could somehow swim off of her lap and escape the fury that was rapidly spreading across her buttocks and thighs. The two of them let themselves be carried away by the hypnotic rhythm of Cassidy's bouncing, burning buns, and Lauren's steady, methodical swatting. Each of them lost in their own little world as the steady *SMACK! SMACK! SMACK!* of Lauren's right palm filled the spaces between their heartbeats.

Without either of them even realizing it was happening, several long minutes had come and gone, and by the time the last two swats found their marks dead center across the meatiest parts of each of Cassidy's cheeks, they were both left panting and exhausted. Covered in a fine sheen of sweat and feeling as if they'd just ran a marathon, the two of them spent several moments catching their breath and gathering their thoughts while Lauren amused herself with rubbing and occasionally pinching her best friend's roasted rear end. Cassidy's backside was now painted a brilliant shade of stop sign red from the crowns of her cheeks, to nearly halfway down her still squirming thighs. Part of Lauren wanted nothing more than to soothe the poor girl, to rub away the sting and kiss her all better, but the way she squeaked and gasped, squirmed and wriggled, whenever she dug her nails into her swollen flesh or traced a fingertip between the two scalded moons upturned over her lap was just too much of a temptation to resist. To say nothing of the glistening moisture that had nothing to do with their sweating or the hot tub they'd been soaking in that she caught glimpses of whenever Cassidy's thighs shifted or parted. That in and of itself was proving to be a *very* tempting target that Lauren had to exercise all of her willpower not to go after right there and then. Despite all that had just happened between the two of them, it was better to take some things a bit slower when it came to that particular part of their budding relationship she suspected.

Eventually enough time passed that it became clear to them both that it was time to move on, and with much reluctance, Lauren helped her friend slide off her thighs and clamber awkwardly back to her feet to stand in front of her, only wobbling a little bit with the effort. Being released from her best friend's lap seemed to have broken the spell that they'd both been under for the last few minutes, and Cassidy found herself staring into the eyes of her roommate. She was shocked to find that instead of its usual confidence, Lauren's gaze held uncertainty and doubt as she looked up at her from her spot still sitting on the pool lounger. Cassidy knew that her eyes too probably held much the same look, but in that moment something in the back of her mind that had been brewing for months finally clicked into place and she decided to throw caution to the wind once more. It had served her well so far, so why not keep it going?

With her best approximation of Lauren's usual half-grin, she stooped forward and shuffled out of the swimsuit still clinging to her ankles, before popping back up again and facing her with her hands on her hips. Then, before her courage could fail her, she closed the distance between the two of them, and with a slight hiss through clenched teeth, plopped herself down onto the older girl's lap, deliberately straddling her legs to either side of her and wrapping them around her waist. Feeling herself blushing both from her own sudden boldness, and embarrassment at the little gasps that kept escaping her lips whenever she shifted her weight around on Lauren's lap, Cassidy leaned in close and planted her lips on her best friend's for the most passionate kiss she could muster.

"Thanks for that," she finally managed to say sometime later when she pulled away from Lauren, flashing her a bashful grin.

"You're very welcome," purred Lauren, letting the hands that had wrapped themselves around her best friend's shoulders slide casually down her back to take up two handfuls of still-sizzling cheek. "It looks like I finally found your love language, cutie pie."

Blushing all over again and smiling from ear to ear, her heart fluttering with more delight than she would have thought possible at hearing her best friend use the pet name again, Cassidy squirmed in Lauren's grip and nodded. Letting out a squeak of surprise as her nails dug into a particularly tender spot, Cassidy leaned in closer and wrapped her arms around the older girl's shoulders with a sigh.

"Yeah, well, um… maybe just a little…"

"Hah, don't even *try* to pretend you didn't love every second of that just now," growled Lauren, triumphantly digging her fingernails even harder into Cassidy's fleshy cheeks and being rewarded with a fresh round of very satisfying squirming from her. She then pitched her voice into a low conspiratorial whisper and brought her lips right beside the girl's ear to murmur. "I saw what you were watching the other night when you thought I was asleep, you know."

Cassidy in turn pulled back at this revelation, her face going rigid with embarrassment as she spluttered incoherently to try and deny it, leaving her vulnerable for Lauren to move in and plant a kiss of her own onto her pouting lips.

"I hope we get to do this again soon," she said, her face adopting the softest, most genuine smile that Cassidy had ever seen on it. With that confession out in the open, Lauren felt her confidence starting to slip again and hastened to add. "I mean, if that's okay with you and all…"

In response, Cassidy just squeezed her friend nice and tight, beaming.

"Oh yes, please!" she gushed, feeling herself growing bolder by the second. "I'm sure you'll be able to find plenty of excuses to get your hands on my caboose before too long. That is… if you think you can handle it."

Still giddy from all that had just happened, she gave said caboose a meaningful little wriggle that just so happened to grind her wet sex up against her best friend, and now possibly more's waist, and giggled. She then, with much reluctance, awkwardly disentangled herself from around her and climbed back to her feet, before leaning in for one last quick peck on the lips.

"But first, I think you and I ought to finish off those ciders in the hot tub. I'm freezing!"

And with that, she spun on her heel and dashed off to canon ball right into the center of the Jacuzzi spa, splashing water everywhere and giggling up a storm. Heedless of the white bikini bottoms she'd left abandoned at Lauren's feet.

It was a *very* good night for them both.

Chapter 2

Things Come to a Boil

Despite the precedent that had been set by the hot tub incident and Cassidy's valiant attempts to goad her roommate into putting her back over her knee again for another round, while of course pretending that that wasn't at all what she was trying to do in the slightest, the next few days passed by uneventfully for the two of them. Of course Cassidy's sudden upswing in smart-ass comments, her blasting her music at a volume that was *just* loud enough to be annoying, and the proliferation of random bits of clothing and snack wrappers popping up in small groups of twos and threes all over the apartment in places where they'd be sure to get in the way and irk her highly organized roommate did not go unnoticed by Lauren. But even so, she deliberately refused to take the other girl's bait; no matter how enticing it was whenever she waggled it at her when she thought she wasn't looking. Instead she savored Cassidy's mounting frustrations as they grew more and more apparent with each failed attempt to coax her into action, knowing full well how much her inaction was driving the other girl crazy.

Truth be told, Lauren wanted nothing more than to haul her best friend, and now possible girlfriend, over her lap for a repeat performance of what had happened by the pool that night at her aunt and uncle's house, but she forced herself to be patient, to wait. She knew that Cassidy wanted her to spank her again, and she desperately wanted to as well, but there was something inside of her, some innate understanding of the power dynamic developing between the two of them that held her back. It was an instinct that whispered to her that it would be far more effective and meaningful for them both if it was *her*, not Cassidy, who was the one to decide where and when the next spanking took place. After all, *she* was the hunter in their little game of cat and mouse, not her roommate, and she could hardly think of herself as the one in control if she pounced at every little provocation so brazenly laid out in front of her, now could she? So she let the other girl's sass slide, only ever meeting it with her usual response of a raised eyebrow or a sharp look, though now occasionally coupled with a pinch or pat to her cheeks whenever she wasn't paying attention. Even so, she was very careful to never actually make a move toward properly punishing her. At least, not yet.

That all changed a few days later, just as Cassidy was changing into her pajamas in preparation for several more hours of playing around on her computer and watching TV before thinking about maybe heading for bed. She was a natural-born night owl after all, and while she didn't have any plans to hit the hay before 2 AM came and went, that didn't mean she couldn't be comfortable in the meantime. Lauren just so happened to be passing by the slightly ajar door to her bedroom, on her way to her own room in search of where she'd left her tablet, when she caught sight of her roommate changing into her pajamas. Cassidy tended to be a bit shy when it came to dressing and undressing in front of her still, despite Lauren's total lack of self-consciousness when it came to her own nudity, and so she was reasonably sure that the impromptu show she was putting on for her as she hopped from foot to foot wriggling her pajama bottoms up over the swell of her hips wasn't an intentional one. Even so, the sight of her adorable caboose bobbing from side to side, all but demanding she yank her pajama bottoms down and slap it silly, sent an electric thrill down Lauren's spine and she knew that her moment had finally come. She took a second to fully commit to memory the sight of those baby-blue horizontal stripes tracing across the curves of her best friend's cheeks as they disappeared beneath a pair of plaid pajama pants, before straightening to her full height and moving in to strike.

"Oh Cassie," she called, not bothering to knock as she pushed her roommate's door all the way open and confidently strolled into the ordered chaos that was her bedroom. Keeping her face straight and fixing her with her best "you're in trouble" glare, she all but pinned the other girl in place where she'd fallen back to perch on the edge of her bed as she frowned. "You and I need to talk."

An intense flood of emotions washed over Cassidy as her cheeks involuntarily clenched beneath her. On the one hand, she still felt giddy whenever her roommate used one of the handful of pet names she'd cooked up for her over the course of the last week, but on the other she sensed that they were about to have a serious discussion. Immediately fears that her friend was about to say that the last time she'd spanked her was a mistake and that they should never do it again, or even worse, that she thought they should move out and find other people to live with, flooded through her, twisting her stomach into harsh knots as her heartbeat thudded in her ears.

"Um, uh…" she gulped. "Sure, Lauren. Um, what's up?"

Lauren picked up almost immediately on the sudden flood

of anxiety that had spread across her best friend's face, but resisted the urge to reassure her just yet. Instead she savored the anticipation she'd been kindling for the last few days a little bit longer, knowing full well that what she had planned would wipe away the girl's doubts far more effectively than a couple of vocal reassurances and a pat on the shoulder ever could. And so, suppressing a grin, she took a few steps closer until she was looming over Cassidy with her hands planted firmly on her hips as she glowered down at her, and then sprang her trap.

"I think you and I both know that the way you've been behaving these past few days has been totally unacceptable."

She kept her voice stern, but let the corner of her mouth twitch up in a quick half-grin that gave away how she really felt. Not that Cassidy was in much of a position to pick up on her roommate's subtle facial tics at that particular moment.

"I'm sick and tired of you thinking you can get away with murder around here. You've been a huge brat all week, and it stops *now*. Do you hear me?"

In spite of the fact that her entire lecture was totally off the cuff, being made up as she went along mostly from half-re-membered bits and pieces from her own run ins with pissed off parents, Lauren couldn't help but be impressed with herself just a little bit. She sounded just the perfect amount of grumpy and fed up that she'd been aiming for, and if the indignant look of confusion that had replaced the worry on Cassidy's face was anything to go by, she'd hit her mark dead center.

"Wha- But I haven't-!" she began to protest, before Lauren cut her off.

"Uh-uh. Don't you *dare* try and sweet talk your way out

of this, missy," she snapped, raising a hand to forestall any more arguments from her friend before they could come out. "You've more than earned the trip across my knee you're about to take, and unless you want to spend the next week going to bed with a well-cooked ass, I'd start changing my tune."

Still reeling from the whiplash of emotions she'd just experienced, Cassidy let the fear that she'd somehow ruined things between her and Lauren fall away from her as if it'd never been there in the first place. With a sigh of relief, feeling much more sure-footed in their relationship than she had just a few moments earlier, she realized all too late that she'd been expertly painted into a corner by her smugly smirking probably-girlfriend. And yet, she found herself grinning right back up at her as she let herself slip comfortably into the role of sassy brat hurtling toward her inevitable date with a sore bottom.

"Honestly, a week doesn't really sound all that terrible if you ask me," she quipped, deliberately leaning back to rest her palms behind her on the bed with indifference as she rolled her eyes.

Lauren felt the corners of her mouth twitch up at that, and she had to fight hard to suppress a laugh. Eventually she managed to twist her amusement into something more predatory as she bore her teeth in a wolfish grin that she knew would send thigh-squirming chills down Cassidy's spine.

"Well then, miss smart mouth," she said, her voice menacingly casual as if it didn't matter to her one way or the other as she called the other girl's bluff. "We'll just have to see how confident you're feeling after I've finished with whooping that bratty little butt of yours raw with my belt. That is to say, *after* we've finished with the spanking you've already got coming, of course."

"Raw?" countered Cassidy, feigning confusion even as she felt a pit open up in the bottom of her stomach. She could feel herself blushing hot pink and it was suddenly a lot harder to sound smug as she plowed ahead with her come back, unable to resist the urge to dig herself in just a little bit deeper. "I thought you said I was going to be 'well-cooked' by the time you were through with me. Make up your mind already, geez."

That little outburst of bold-faced sass managed to at least make Lauren snort.

"Oh that is *it*. Get over here you little brat!" she growled, unable to totally keep the amusement out of her voice as she snatched Cassidy up from the bed by her wrist. She replaced her a split-second later with a bounce and wasted no time in hauling the startled girl across her lap, centering her pajama-clad butt across the top of her right thigh and faceplanting her into the heavy down comforter while her feet scrabbled frantically for purchase just a few inches above the carpet. "I don't care what you want to call it, you're getting *spanked*!"

Fueled by a vindictive determination to give her best friend everything she'd been asking for and more, Lauren immediately set to work walloping her oh-so-deserving backside with a vengeance. She kept the fingers of her right hand tight together and her thumb out to the side as she brought her palm down with the same relentlessly powerful swats that she'd used the last time she'd had Cassidy over her knee, setting a nearly non-stop tempo that the other girl's flailing feet had no problem keeping up with. Unlike last time though, Cassidy at least had the good fortune to be wearing more than just a wet swimsuit for protection, and the soft material of her pajama bottoms managed to deaden the noise of Lauren's palm quite a bit as it bounced off the back of them, absorbing most of the sting from the individual spanks but doing very little to lessen the bone-jarring impact that the heel of her palm brought with it, bouncing Cassidy forward and all but knocking a squeak of surprise from her each time it struck home.

Nearly three dozen spanks later, Lauren paused a moment to give her aching palm a break. She was starting to see where the old adage of "this is going to hurt me more than it hurts you" might have come from, because pounding her palm against those deceptively tough pajamas seemed to be having more of an effect on her than it did on her roommate. She would *definitely* be starting off any and all future spankings over her panties, or straight to her bare bottom, that was for sure. Not wanting to give away just how she was feeling right then though, she was aiming for a sense of dominant control after all, Lauren masked her need for a breather by rubbing her stinging palm in slow, smooth circles across the tautly stretched seat of Cassidy's pajama bottoms. With a grin of anticipation, mentally picturing what lay hidden just beneath their surface, she searched out the raised stitching that marked the edge of Cassidy's panties and began to casually trace her fingertips along it. Starting from where the material clung snugly to the side of her hip, she swept her touch down and in along the prominent undercurve of her right cheek, raking her index and middle fingers across the point where it disappeared into her crack and letting her touch linger and rub for a few extra moments between her thighs before following the divide between her cheeks up to her waistband and giving her rump a playful slap.

"Am I starting to make an impression on you yet, cutie pie?" demanded Lauren, her voice a low purr as she gave Cassidy's right cheek a hard enough squeeze to make her gasp.

"Y-Yeah sure, I guess," Cassidy managed to answer back with a huff, blowing a strand of curly blonde hair out of her face and managing to give a convincing enough shrug, knowing full well how her roommate would respond to it.

"Good," crooned Lauren, her voice syrupy sweet as she took the bait. "Now raise your hips."

That order sent a shiver of fear down Cassidy's spine, and she found herself swallowing the smart-ass reply that had been on the tip of her tongue just a second earlier as she hastened to do as she was told. Unfortunately for her, her feet were still suspended several inches above the floor, and any attempts she made to try and find purchase with her toes were fruitless as they bobbed uselessly back and forth in the air.

"Um...?"

Lauren just smirked to herself as she watched the show for a bit, before eventually taking matters into her own hands, literally.

"Come here you," she said, heaving out a put upon sigh as she leaned in to snake her left arm around Cassidy's waist, pulling the other girl in firmly against her side and lifting her hips clear off of her lap with ease.

Cradling her in the crook of her arm, Lauren let the reality of her friend's new position sink in for her before she reached beneath her to pull her pajama drawstring free. The knot came away with ease, Cassidy never tied anything more complicated than a simple bow with bunny ears to keep her pajamas from slipping down to embarrass her, and with the waistband of her pajamas now considerably less snug, Lauren was able to easily drag them down off of her hips, along her legs, and then off entirely. With an intense feeling of satisfaction at how easily that had gone, she was pleased to find she had a natural talent for undressing her friend, she tossed the no longer needed pajama pants in the general direction of Cassidy's clothes hamper, making the shot without even trying, and then turned her attention back to the pair of panties she'd just unveiled. She was more than a little gratified to find that the mental snapshot she'd taken just before bursting into her room was an accurate one, the inch-wide horizontal stripes she'd caught only a short glimpse of were stretched snugly across her seat and did indeed outline every contour of the generous cheeks they were wrapped around in explicit detail, though their gusset now sported a very visible damp spot that hadn't been there earlier.

"These are cute and all," quipped Lauren, not bothering to mask the mounting hunger in her voice as she spoke, admiring the feel of her friend's cheeks through the soft cotton material as they shifted nervously beneath her rubbing. "But I think you and I both know that there's no way I'm going to let you keep them on. Not after the way you've been behaving, Cassie dear, so I'm afraid they're just going to *have* to come off."

"Ugh, fine, *whatever*," grumbled Cassidy, only able to muster the barest semblance of a protest as she felt Lauren's free hand strip away the last bit of protection between her and the cool air of her bedroom and what was to come, squirming and flexing her now naked cheeks as she felt more than heard the other girl ball up her embarrassingly wet panties and toss them into the hamper after her pajamas with careless ease. Despite the indignant pout on her blushing face, Cassidy loved every moment of what was happening to her. She knew instinctively that Lauren wouldn't have let her keep her panties, even if she'd properly whined about it, and even as her tummy filled with dread and her mind reeled at how easily she'd been manhandled and stripped of her pajamas and panties, leaving her bare bottomed and waiting for what was sure to be a very intense spanking if last time was anything to go by, she found her heart welling with a heady mixture of eager anticipation and a sense of intense closeness with her friend.

No, Cassidy mused to herself, time seeming to draw to a standstill for a handful of heartbeats as the world suddenly snapped into greater focus around her. It was safe to say that in that moment, they'd moved well and truly beyond being just "friends", or even "best friends", they were definitely deep into girlfriend territory now, and probably had been for several weeks already, though neither of them had been ready to put a label on it quite yet. And although it wasn't at all the traditional path one might take toward starting a relationship, she wouldn't have had it any other way as she sighed with a contentment she'd never felt before.

Lauren's own thoughts seemed to have been traveling along a similar trajectory too, for it was in that very next moment as she was settling Cassidy back down across her lap and testing the feel of her bare cheeks in her palms that she said it.

"I love you, cutie pie."

Neither of them really knew what to say as they let those five words hang in the air for several long moments, but eventually Cassidy broke the tension with a saucy squirm of her seat.

"I love you too, bossy boots."

And with that, her heart fuller than it had been in a very long time, Lauren set to work showing her girlfriend just how much she loved her. This time around, she kept her pace nice and slow, savoring the sound and sensations of her palm impacting with Cassidy's bare skin and watching with delight as it bounced and jiggled. More often than not, she'd follow up a particularly vicious swat with an equally hard squeeze, digging her fingernails in deep against the sensitive flesh she'd just sizzled. She'd then give it a rough shake that set the other girl's ass to jiggling in a way that was different from when she slapped it, but was just as satisfying, before letting go and repeating the process all over again somewhere else. Every now and then though she couldn't resist kicking things up a notch, and would jolt Cassidy out of her quiet submission with a dozen hard, stinging smacks in a wide arc up and down her bottom and thighs, much to the other girl's dismay if her cries of surprise and squeals of pain were any indication.

The slower pace did very little to effect the severity of the punishment being dished out however, and after a long and thorough spanking, Cassidy's poor backside was just as sore and red as it had been the last time she'd found herself across Lauren's knee. Once the punishment was finally over, the two of them spent several long and wonderful moments in a companionable silence, mostly. Although she was no longer spanking, Lauren kept her hands busy rubbing and squeezing her girlfriend's cherry-red derriere, admiring her handiwork and savoring the heat radiating from her in more places than one. Occasionally she'd let her fingertips venture further south to ever so lightly graze along the wet and swollen lips pouting up at her from between Cassidy's thighs, though she never let them linger for long despite the sharp intake of breath and high-pitched gasps their attention always brought.

After a while doing this, Lauren leaned over and casually

brushed back several strands of sweaty blonde hair that had plastered themselves to her girlfriend's forehead, tucking them behind her ear and beaming fondly down at her with a mixture of affection and something more predatory. She then leaned over, and with her lips tickling the side of her ear, murmured with sadistic mirth.

"Now if you'd been a good girl and taken your spanking without all that sass, we'd be wrapping up your time over my knee tonight with some of *this*."

She illustrated just what exactly she meant by "this" as she let the fingers of her right hand caress themselves along her slit, gliding up and down along its moist folds several times before stopping to rub them in in tight circles around her throbbing clit. Cassidy's face immediately buried itself in her comforter as she bit out a long, low moan, her legs jutting out straight behind her as if they'd just been shocked by lighting before starting to squirm frantically as she rapidly approached the edge of a climax. Keeping a sharp eye on the other girl's body language, Lauren kept it up until right before she was sure she was about to come, and then snatched her hand away, chuckling darkly and dishing out two extra sharp thigh spanks to add insult to injury.

"Oh my god, Lauren, come on!" whined Cassidy, pounding her fists ineffectually against her mattress and scissoring her ankles back and forth behind her in an attempt to try and finish the job herself. Unfortunately with her feet still suspended several inches off the floor, she couldn't find the leverage she needed, and with a loud huff, let herself go limp across her girlfriend's lap in defeat.

"Maybe next time, cutie pie," teased Lauren, tucking away the adorable vision of Cassidy rosy rumped across her lap and pouting adorably with her chin perched atop her folded arms for later when she had some alone time with her magic wand. "But for now, *you* have a date with my belt I believe."

This announcement set off another round of moaning and grumbling from Cassidy, but it was clear that her frustration was decidedly less genuine this time around as Lauren gave her naked seat a couple of casually possessive pats before helping her back to her feet. She held her there in front of her for a few long moments, pinned in place by the force of her wry half-smirk alone, drinking in the sight of her as she shifted her weight awkwardly from foot to foot with her hands balled into little fists at her sides. She was pouting just as hard as she possibly could at her, bare from the waist down and proving definitively that she was indeed a natural blonde as Lauren had suspected, but to her credit she made no move to cover herself or to try and wheedle her way out of what she still had coming.

Heaving out a long suffering sigh as if she'd rather be doing anything else right then, though they both knew that that was totally not the case at all, Lauren rose gracefully from her perch on the side of the bed and took a moment to straighten out her own clothes. Deliberately adjusting a cuff here, smoothing out a wrinkle there, all but ignoring the other girl even as she underscored for her just who was in charge at that moment and who was the brat about to get her ass strapped raw. Or was it well-cooked? They'd find out for sure which it was in a minute or two. Turning her back on Cassidy, she leaned over her mattress and busied herself for several more moments carefully smoothing out the wrinkles their previous activities had left in the covers, before gathering up the three pillows at the head of her bed and stacking them in a neat pile near its center. After taking a moment to appraise her arrangement, Lauren shook her head with dissatisfaction, something was missing. She then reached over and snatched up the worn teddy bear Cassidy kept beside her pillows, the one she'd received on her sixth birthday and that had been with her ever since, and set it just in front of her pillow pile where she'd have easy access to it. Perfect.

"Lay across these," she ordered, patting the pillows almost fondly before taking a step back to watch with naked amusement while she tapped her forefinger against the rounded silver hoop of her belt buckle.

Her wolfish grin grew even wider at the visible shiver that ran down Cassidy's spine as her gaze shifted from the bed, to her tapping finger, and then up to her face, making her cheeks wobble and painting a fresh blush across her face in the process. Clearly embarrassed by the extra display her lack of clothing was providing for her girlfriend, she gave a huff of defiance and tried to suppress her visible nervousness as she moved to do as she was told. Faster than she would have liked, Cassidy found herself lying face down across her mattress with her already sore and bright-red bottom propped up high behind her, just *begging* to be spanked.

Still grinning from ear to ear, Lauren casually undid the buckle of her belt and began to slide it free from around her waist, savoring the "thwip, thwip, thwip" sounds it made as it snaked free from its loops.

"I think we'll just stick with twelve for tonight," she said, doubling the length of leather up in her hands and giving it a few sharp snaps that made Cassidy jump in spite of herself, much to Lauren's amusement. She just loved the way her girl-friend's ass jiggled and bounced at the slightest provocation. "I *suspect* you can take a whole lot more than twelve if I'm being honest, but for now, let's keep things simple. I'm *sure* we'll get the chance to put my little theory to the test sooner rather than later."

In spite of the stomach-churning nervousness gripping her guts and pulsing between her legs, Cassidy found that part of her was a little disappointed to hear that she'd only be getting twelve licks of Lauren's belt that night. Her girlfriend was definitely right about her being able to take more. Her ass had shown no signs of even so much as a friendly slap the following morning after they'd been hot tubbing, and the two dozen or so times her parents had spanked her while growing up had been pretty much the same as well. Having a jiggly rear end that could absorb a lot of punishment certainly had its perks, although she resisted the urge to say that out loud just then.

SWISH-CRACK!

Cassidy's idly spinning thoughts were immediately cut short by Lauren's belt as it hissed through the air and exploded across the crowns of her cheeks. Its echoing report was accompanied by a howl of surprise from her as a one-inch wide bar of white-hot fury spread across where the leather had just bit into her already tender flesh, raising a vivid red welt in its place and burning fiercely for several agonizing moments before burrowing deeper into her and fading only slightly into a broader, pulsating ache. Lauren mercifully let Cassidy ride out the worst of the pain of that first lick while she caught her breath, savoring the sight of her toes curling and uncurling as her hands gripped her comforter in a white-knuckled fury. Cassidy was starting to think that maybe she'd been just a *bit* cocky in her earlier estimations of how much she could take from just a moment ago, and as she finally managed to take in a breath that wasn't hissed through clenched teeth, the next swat found its mark just below the first.

SWISH-CRACK!

On and on Lauren worked, methodically painting stripe after vivid red stripe that quickly rose into angry red welts up and down all along the alluring expanse of Cassidy's cheeks and the backs of her thighs. She resisted the urge to rush ahead with the girl's punishment, and instead took her time to carefully aim each of her stripes, savoring the impact of her belt against her girlfriend's soft skin and the accompanying squeal of pain it wrought from her tossed back head as her legs thrashed her mattress in a futile attempt to throw off some of the agony she was experiencing. The thigh swats in particular drew extra loud cries of pain from her, but even though it was obvious that she was on the verge of bursting into tears at any moment, she never once asked her to stop. Lauren knew that the other girl trusted her completely, and she was determined to push her right up to her limit, and maybe even a little past it, but no further. And so she kept a sharp eye on Cassidy's body language, instinctively understanding what she was really feeling with each movement of her hips and the arching of her back, and adjusted the strength of her swats accordingly, never going easy on her, but never pushing things too far either.

By the time it was all over, nearly a quarter of an hour had passed, and Cassidy's bottom and thighs were left painted a lurid shade of bright, candy apple red with darker patches of maroon splashed almost haphazardly all along their surface in sharp, crisscrossing lines. She could feel the hard, raised edges of the welts left behind by Lauren's belt throbbing in time with the beating of her heart, echoing the pain of each previous impact as they pulsed their heat deeper and deeper into her aching sex. With a jolt of embarrassment, she felt the wet spot she'd left on the pillow she was lying across, and in that moment she wanted nothing more than to plunge her hands beneath her to finish what Lauren had started, but she resisted that urge knowing that to do so would almost certainly invite more licks of that damn belt of hers.

Lauren for her part was having just as much trouble resisting the temptation to attend to her own body's demands just then, and she busied her hands with fumbling her belt back through its loops and pulling it tight across her waist while she kept her eyes fixated on Cassidy's bare ass and legs. It was taking a supreme effort of will for her to not pounce on the girl just then, to viciously squeeze those battered buns of hers and make her howl, to pull them apart and bury her face between her legs, but somehow she resisted. She knew that there would be plenty of time for those kinds of things in the future, and while she would have loved to claim her prize and rock the other girl's world until the sun came up and they had to rush to class, denying her and leaving her frustrated and bone-achingly sore was even more fun. She did however indulge herself just a little bit as she reached out and gave Cassidy's right cheek a hard slap that elicited a *very* satisfying yelp. She was only human after all.

Chuckling to herself, Lauren moved in to sit down on the edge of the bed once again, scooting over and tugging away some pillows so that Cassidy's head could rest in her lap as she turned over to lay on her side with a low groan. They spent several quiet moments just enjoying the feel of each other's warmth, not really saying anything in particular as Lauren busied herself with rubbing the other girl's back and gently tucking away sweaty locks of hair behind her ear. It was pretty clear though that Cassidy was down for the count, and if the way her hands kept twitching towards her middle were any indication, she was in desperate need of some alone time. Truth be told, Lauren was in more than a little need of some of that herself, and so deciding it was time to part ways for the evening, she dipped her head down and planted a quick kiss on her girlfriend's cheek.

And with that, Lauren disentangled herself from Cassidy and rose to her feet one last time. As she moved to leave, her mind already replaying scenes from the last half hour as her hands itched to get hold of her magic wand, she turned back and smiled wistfully at the back of the girl she wanted so badly to climb under the covers with. She knew there would be plenty of opportunities for that in the future though, and so she contented herself with committing to memory the sight of her swollen red ass as Cassidy lay on her side groping it tentatively with one hand while her other busied itself elsewhere.

"Goodnight Cassie, I love you."

"Me too," squeaked Cassidy, too far gone into her own ministrations to do much more than look back over her shoulder and flash her a quick, embarrassed grin.

It was going to be a long night.

Chapter 3

Laundry Layabout

After sending her girlfriend to bed frustrated to the point of near hysterics and nursing a throbbing behind that was somehow simultaneously both raw *and* well-cooked, spanking quickly became a regular part of Lauren and Cassidy's day-to-day routine. Now that the ice had been broken between the two of them with regard to their new dynamic, and they'd proven to themselves that what had happened that night by the pool *hadn't* been a fluke, it seemed that barely a day went by that Lauren didn't find some excuse or another to get her hands on her roommate's adorable little caboose. Usually Cassidy would say something sassy that she knew would annoy her girlfriend, or she might get caught up in a game on her phone and not be listening when she tried asking her a question, and of course there was her near-perpetual habit of forgetting to toss out her empty soda cans or put her dirty dishes in the sink that always drove Lauren up the wall. All fairly minor things on their own, but more than enough of an excuse for her to take advantage of whenever the opportunity presented itself.

Once Cassidy had nudged her toe just a bit too far over the line, Lauren would spring into action. She'd pluck her phone from her hands and fix her with a grumpy scowl, or quirk an eyebrow at her and glower whenever she thought she was being clever, and the sudden look of apprehension and looming worry that spread across the other girl's face would make it all too clear that she knew exactly what was about to happen next. Lauren would then grab Cassidy by the scruff of her neck, prop her left foot up on any conveniently low enough nearby surface and drape her girlfriend across her raised knee. If no such suitable spot were available when it was spanking time, she'd usually just make do with tucking Cassidy under her arm as if she were a sack of potatoes, holding her suspended in the air with her left arm cinched tight around her waist like a steel vice. Cassidy would then immediately start to protest that Lauren was being unfair or that this really wasn't necessary, only to groan in embarrassment as she felt her skirt being flipped up or her pants unceremoniously yanked down off of her round hips. Her frantic whining would then suddenly shift into yelps of surprise and squeals of pain as Lauren's palm started exploding against the seat of her panties, hard and fast.

Since the causes for these little impromptu discipline sessions were always minor things, Lauren intentionally kept her reprisals on the lighter side as well. She'd usually just dish out about three dozen or so swats to her girlfriend's wriggling panty-clad rump, always enjoying getting to see the cute pairs of underwear she kept in rotation, or if her pants coming down had managed to partway yank down her panties as well, then it was bare bottom for her. All in all, the spankings themselves weren't particularly harsh. They were essentially just an excuse for Lauren to embarrass her girlfriend, to reinforce just who was in charge in their relationship, and to get her all hot and bothered, before just as quickly setting her back on her feet and sending her on her way as if nothing had just happened.

Of course that isn't to say that Lauren wasn't dishing out more prolonged and intense spankings from time to time as well. While she certainly capitalized on any chance she might get to dust off the back of her girlfriend's panties, she always kept a sharp eye out for any chance to "properly" discipline Cassidy that might come her way as well. And while those opportunities were certainly rarer than the more plentiful excuses for "attitude adjusters" were, Cassidy still managed to find herself going to bed with a fire-engine red rear end about once a week. Sometimes more if she were unlucky, or just feeling extra frisky.

In fact, one such opportunity presented itself just a few days after Lauren and Cassidy had first said "I love you" to each other.

—

Pulling open the rickety false-wood doors next to their refrigerator that hid the tiny laundry alcove from the rest of the apartment, Lauren set her basket of dirty clothes down on top of the dryer and moved to throw back the lid of their washing machine. What greeted her as the metal panel pivoted upward was the sight of wet clothes clumped together and clinging to the bottom of the washing drum, sopping wet and reeking of mildew. Wrinkling her nose at the unpleasant smell wafting up at her, Lauren suddenly found herself both annoyed at having to deal with a delay in doing her laundry, again, and elated that a golden opportunity to *really* tear her girlfriend's bottom up had just dropped into her lap.

"Cassie!" she snapped, loud enough for the other girl to hear her all the way back in her bedroom with her music pumping as she whirled around from the laundry machine with a low growl. "You'd better get your butt in here right now, missy!"

Cassidy for her part could immediately sense that something was up when she heard Lauren calling for her. If nothing else, her tone made it pretty clear that she'd just stumbled onto something that had ticked her off but good, and not something Cassidy had meant for her to stumble across either. Swallowing hard, her mouth suddenly dry and her face flushed hot pink, she quickly said goodbye to the friends she'd been chatting with online, saved her progress on her homework, paused her music, and then sprung to her feet. Despite the pressing worry that any more delays would only make things worse for her, Cassidy couldn't help but linger with her hand on her doorknob as she stared at herself in the mirror beside her dresser. She spent a few precious heartbeats casting a critical eye over her reflection, and after making a couple quick adjustments to her hair and straightening her glasses, she threw open her bedroom door and all but sprinted into the kitchen where she found Lauren waiting for her with her arms folded under her expansive chest and an annoyed scowl plastered across her face.

"Did you need something, hon?" asked Cassidy, doing her best to sound nonchalant and only panting a little bit. Why was it so hot all of a sudden? Was the heater on?

"You wouldn't happen to remember how long ago it was that you started doing your laundry, now would you?" demanded Lauren, arching a critical eyebrow at her roommate and turning to point at the smelly pile of wet clothes at the bottom of the laundry machine.

Stepping in closer and leaning over the edge of the machine

to get a good look at what Lauren was pointing at, Cassidy felt a pit open up in the bottom of her stomach, draining the color from her face as she frantically tried to figure out just how long she'd left her laundry sitting there for.

"Oh shoot! Um… like, maybe a couple of days… ish?"

She could already feel herself starting to squirm with dread as the by now familiar combo of stomach-clenching fear and anticipation started to wriggle itself between her legs and up her spine.

"A couple *days?*" echoed Lauren, not sounding impressed at all. She let the lid of the washing machine slam shut behind her as she rounded on the other girl with her hands on her hips.

"I think so!" squeaked Cassidy, jumping with the sudden loud *CLANK!* of metal on metal and inadvertently putting a crack in her girlfriend's angry mask as the corner of her mouth twitched up in a smirk.

"You think so?" repeated Lauren in a slow deadpan voice, fixing her roommate with a hard stare and watching with barely concealed amusement as she squirmed nervously under the force of her glare.

"Yeah… I'm sorry. I guess it just sort of slipped my mind, my bad…"

"Hmmm, your bad huh?" smiled Lauren, going from frosty to way too casual in the blink of an eye. "Well, I *think* that since you can't even be sure just how long ago it was that you started doing your laundry, that neither of us can be one hundred percent sure that what you're wearing now is all that clean either."

"In fact," she continued, stepping in closer and tracing a

fingertip down along her girlfriend's jawline before tipping her head back so that she had to look her in the eye. "I think it would be best if you took all these clothes you're wearing off."

Lauren kept her grip on Cassidy's brightly blushing chin and leaned forward to plant a quick, but commanding kiss on her lips, before adding in a steely voice that made it abundantly clear that she wasn't making a suggestion.

"*Now.*"

"But-!" Cassidy began to protest, balling her hands into little fists at her sides and stomping her right foot before she'd even realized she was doing it.

"Cassie." Lauren cut her off by gently pressing the tip of her index finger to her lips. She kept her voice deceptively casual, but the glint in her eye and the predatory smirk on her face made it very clear just how thin the ice was that her girlfriend was now treading on. "You're already in enough trouble as it is, cutie pie. Do you *really* want to make me repeat myself?"

Cassidy's knee-jerk reaction to this was of course that yes, yes she did indeed want to see what making her grumpy girlfriend repeat herself would get her, but at that moment her eyes just so happened to flick down from her grinning face to catch sight of the wide leather belt wrapped snugly around her waist, and whatever smart-ass remark she'd been preparing to throw back at her died in her throat with a strangled squeak. She remembered all too well just how much that belt had hurt on her bare bottom only a handful of days ago, and couldn't help but shiver as Lauren's ominous promise of seeing how many more licks she could take echoed in her ears. Twelve had been bad enough as it was, and as much fun as poking the bear was, she wasn't quite ready for a repeat taste of Lauren's belt just yet. Not today at least.

"That's what I thought," crooned Lauren, all smiles and smug satisfaction as she took a step back to cast an appraising look up and down her girlfriend's body. "Now *strip*."

Blushing furiously and wanting desperately to fire back with something sharp and biting, but unable to think of anything right then that wouldn't just make her sound silly, Cassidy settled for pouting hard at her tormentor before reluctantly beginning to fumble with the clasp on her jeans. It took a couple of tries for her to manage to free her button clasp from its little cloth hook, and as it came free Cassidy could feel that stomach-clenching tension of hers starting to ratchet up several notches. Swallowing hard, she loosened her zipper, and with a fresh blush that did not go unnoticed by Lauren, wriggled and shimmied her hips until they eventually came free of the tight embrace of denim that had been clinging to them just a moment ago. For several agonizingly long heartbeats she just stood there, frozen in time as the reality of what she had coming started to dawn on her, rooted in place before her girlfriend in the middle of their kitchen in her half-zipped navy-blue hoodie and dark gray tank top, black cotton panties with hot pink stitching on full display, and her skinny jeans at half-mast around her knees.

"Oh my god, those are *so* cute," cooed Lauren, breaking Cassidy's trance as she pointed at her panties and smiled. "Please tell me you've got a matching bra on!"

"Ugh, I do..." grumbled Cassidy, unable to fully suppress a chagrinned half-smirk of her own as she rested a hand on the edge of their laundry machine for balance and kicked her skinny jeans off at Lauren's feet. Heaving out a sigh and flashing the other girl a quick wink, she quickly stripped off her hoodie and tank top, dropping them both at her feet as well.

"Tuh-duh," she proclaimed, spreading her fingers wide and waggling her hands out to either side of her in a half-hearted bit of showmanship.

"Oh, my, god, Cassie you are, *adorable*."

Cassidy felt her own smile widen a bit at the sincere praise being lavished on her, though the look in her girlfriend's eyes only made the twisting in her stomach worse.

"Now lose em'."

Folding under the weight of Lauren's expectant stare, Cassidy's blush returned with a vengeance and she reached behind her to unclasp her bra. It slipped from her shoulders with ease, and fell to her feet where it was soon joined by her panties as she kicked them off to join the rest of her clothes.

"Very good," smiled Lauren, taking in the erect nipples peeking out from behind where Cassidy's arms were trying to hide them, and the neatly trimmed thicket of golden curls waving at her from between her squirming thighs. She let the other girl stew for a few moments longer than was strictly necessary, and then gestured down at the small pile of still-warm clothes at her feet, her face taking on a decidedly cruel smirk as she did so. "Now pick those up and throw them in with the rest of your dirty clothes. You'll be staying like that until the washer's finished with them, and the dryer has them nice and warm."

"Fine," grumbled Cassidy, not quite managing to meet her girlfriend's eye as she huffed to herself. Bending over, she quickly gathered up her discarded clothes and threw them into the washer on top of her other ones, tossing in a detergent pod after them before moving to close the lid again.

"Don't forget the fabric softener," teased Lauren, watching with naked amusement as Cassidy had to raise up onto her tip toes and half-crawl over the dryer to reach the bottle she'd indicated. She quickly dumped a capful of it into the center of the drum, and with another huff let the lid slam shut.

"Uh-oh... That isn't *attitude* I'm detecting from you, now is it, cutie pie?" asked Lauren sardonically as she moved past her pouting roommate to pluck up the biggest, heaviest, wooden spoon she could find from the ceramic crock beside their stove. "No matter, I've got just the thing to help clear that right up."

Cassidy's knees gave a noticeable tremble as she watched Lauren SMACK the oval head of the wooden spoon sharply against her palm, unable to quite stop herself from wincing at the sound its impact made. Yes indeed, she thought to herself as she chewed absently on her lower lip, that spoon would have no problems whatsoever clearing up her attitude. She could feel it disappearing already!

Closing the distance on her suddenly dry-mouthed room- mate, Lauren took her by the shoulders and effortlessly spun her around to face the washing machine she'd just slammed shut not a moment earlier, and with a light shove between her shoulder blades, tipped her over it. Cassidy let out a small "oomph" and gasped as her tummy and bare breasts came into contact with the way too chilly metal of the machine beneath her. How could something indoors be so *cold*?

"Spread your legs for me, hon," ordered Lauren, sliding the head of her wooden spoon between Cassidy's legs and rapping it back and forth against the insides of her thighs.

Those minor swats stung like the dickens, and increased

the other girl's squirming tenfold as she hastened to obey, parting her legs as wide as she could in an attempt to flee the sharp stinging rapidly turning her inner thighs a light shade of pink.

"Very cute," cooed Lauren, stopping only after a few final, extra-mean swats along the inside of Cassidy's legs. She then let the spoon trail up first one thigh, and then the other, before stopping to rub it along the parted lips of her sex. That certainly got a reaction out of the other girl, but before she could start enjoying it too much, Lauren snatched the spoon away and then brought it back down in two quick snaps to either cheek. "Now you stay like that until I'm finished. Is that clear?"

"Yes, yes, yes, I hear you!" Cassidy hastened to reassure her, frantically waving her tush from side to side as much as her spread-eagle stance would allow her to as she hissed in a breath through clenched teeth. Holy crap that stupid spoon stung *way* more than a hand did.

"Good," snapped Lauren, punctuating her remark with four more hard swats before pausing to rub the spoon in slow circles across her handiwork. "Because if you break position, I'm not going to stop until I've broken this spoon on your butt."

She popped Cassidy half a dozen more times in half as many seconds, and then leaned over to whisper in her ear, tapping the spoon menacingly between her cheeks. "And after that, I'll find something nice and big to fuck this tight little ass of yours with."

That certainly got a reaction from the poor girl as Lauren felt her cheeks clench involuntarily against her spoon. Smiling, she planted a quick kiss on Cassidy's cheek, savoring the mingled looks of fear and morbid curiosity playing across her features as she stood up. "Or maybe I'll just do all that anyway. You're *awfully* cute when you're crying, you know."

Swallowing hard, Cassidy just smiled nervously back at her girlfriend and surreptitiously moved to better plant her feet against the linoleum. While what Lauren had just threatened her with sounded rather enticing, the burning in her rear end and down along the insides of her thighs from the two dozen or so swats she'd gotten so far from that spoon gave her pause, and she quickly decided she'd do her best to stay in position for now. That spoon stung enough as it was already. There was no need to see how much worse it could be with Lauren swinging for the fences.

Seeing that her threats had had the desired results, and only feeling just a little disappointed that she probably wouldn't be able to make good on them, never mind the fact that she wasn't even sure if she even *could* break a wooden spoon across her roommate's soft and jiggly tush without hurting her way more than she ever would want to, Lauren set to work seeing just how much she could make her dance with her legs spread over a shoulder's width apart. Keeping a casual eye on the digital clock display on the front of their microwave, she spent the next five minutes bouncing the head of her wooden spoon with lightning fast elbow and wrist movements against every available inch of her girlfriend's cheeks, the backs of her thighs, the extra-tender insides of her legs, and every now and then tantalizingly close to her swollen and dewy lips.

She knew that if she popped her there, even lightly, that she could get Cassidy to break her position in a heartbeat. But while the prospect of plowing her in her adorable ruby-red rump while she lay bent over and trapped against their washing machine certainly had its appeal, she also knew that it wasn't exactly something she could actually handle quite yet either. Lauren was familiar enough with the realities and mechanics of anal sex to understand that she'd need to ease her lover into that particular area of fun far more gently than that. But even so… there was nothing holding either of them back from taking advantage of the more traditional uses of a strap-on.

And so, with an evil grin spreading wide across her face, Lauren let fly with an abrupt upward swat directly between her girlfriend's legs, and the rest of their afternoon was history.

Chapter 4

Plug-N-Play Arcade Adventure

Between the rigors of attending classes, studying for exams, and just keeping on top of all their homework, Lauren and Cassidy knew all too well just how precious a night off could be. As a result, they tended to seize any chance to go out and have fun together whenever their schedules (and budgets) would allow for it, and as March gave way to April and they found themselves hurtling toward the end of winter semester, they both decided they could use a break. And so, after some discussion over where they'd have the most fun, and a quick check of their finances to make sure they could actually afford to enjoy themselves, they hopped into Lauren's car and drove down to Pinball Jerry's Arcade and Pizzeria.

They'd both driven by the place a handful of times before without ever stopping to check it out. Its unassuming exterior and pot-hole ridden parking lot had always made it seem like a rundown dump, but they'd recently heard good things about it from some of their friends, and as they pushed their way out of the cold and into the confluence of high-tempo arcade game jingles and Top 40 hits being blasted over tinny speakers, they knew they'd made the right call for how to spend their evening. The inside of Pinball Jerry's was an absolute love letter to the video arcades of the late 80s and early 90s. It was lit by a charming combination of warm incandescent bulbs offset by splashes of bright neon that painted the vinyl records adorning the walls in whimsical hues of blue, green, and red. Its floors were a mixture of exposed brick and cheap carpet covered in zany patterns ripped straight from an episode of Saved by the Bell, and the mouth-watering scent of hot pizza hung thick in the air all around them as they approached the front desk and paid for smartcards. The building itself was divided into two distinct sides, one dedicated to prize games like ski-ball and UFO cranes where you could win a small stuffed animal, as well as more modern games like Mario Kart and the latest iteration of Street Fighter. While the other side was populated by a more eclectic mish-mash of retro beat-em-ups, 2D fighting games, and even a few relics from the dawn of the early eighties. These antiques weren't really much more than a novelty since they weren't all that fun to play, but Cassidy and Lauren still thought it was neat to see some of them in person and pretend for a moment that they'd traveled back in time to an idealized version of a bygone era.

After starting the night off in the modern section of the arcade, winning a few tickets here and there and competing at anything that had a multiplayer mode, Lauren and Cassidy decided to take a break and catch their breath in the "restaurant" that sat situated between the two sides of the arcade. Calling the little eatery a restaurant was definitely a stretch considering it was really nothing more than a scant handful of metal and plastic tables and chairs scattered haphazardly in front of a high bar that only served overpriced slices of greasy "artisan" pizza and craft beer. However, while the food itself didn't seem particularly tasty to either of them, the nostalgic atmosphere of the arcade more than made up for it, and they decided to splurge and treat themselves to what was on tap.

"Just so you know, Cassie. You're getting a spanking when

we get home."

Lauren didn't bother to lean in or keep her voice down as she said it. Instead making the declaration with the same casual nonchalance she might have used when asking her girlfriend how her day had gone, or discussing their plans for the weekend, before taking a long pull from the neck of her beer and smirking.

"Oh my god, shhh! Someone might hear you!" hissed Cassidy, nearly choking on the bite of pizza she'd just taken as she kept her eyes trained ahead on her wickedly-smiling girlfriend in front of her so she wouldn't have to know for sure if anybody actually had heard her. The arcade was *far* from empty that evening. There were plenty of people milling about the bar, and even more who seemed to be carrying on loud conversations at the tables around them, and the last thing she needed was for any of them to overhear how she was going to be going to bed with a sore seat that night.

"Oh I wouldn't worry about them," dismissed Lauren with a casual wave of her hand, not bothering to adjust her volume in the slightest. "I'd be *much* more concerned about that cute little butt of yours, and how red it's going to be by the time I'm finished with it if I were you."

"But why am I going to get a spanking?" whined Cassidy, still refusing to tear her gaze away from Lauren as she kicked her feet at her under the table. "I've been good all night!"

Lauren snorted at that.

"Good? Is that what you'd call the way you've been acting ever since you started winning those games?" She made a sharp gesture toward the side of the arcade they'd spent the better part of the last hour in. "And what about all those red shells you kept shooting at me, hmm? Do you really call *stealing* my spot in first place over and over again 'being good'?"

"Oh come on, that was just a little friendly competition," protested Cassidy, unable to quite stop herself from giggling at the memories of Lauren howling in over-exaggerated fury as she lapped her in their final race. "Can't I have another chance, pretty please?"

She'd discovered recently that she could sometimes talk her way, at least partially, out of a spanking if she turned on the charm and threw in a little (or a lot) of begging. It didn't always work, and more often than not it backfired in spectacular ways that left her sore well into the next morning, but that just made it all the more fun as far as she was concerned.

"Hmmm, well…" Lauren pretended to think about it as she took a bite of her own slice of pizza and washed it down with another pull from her beer.

There was no way she was going to let Cassidy off without a spanking. It had been way, way too long since she'd really made her girlfriend howl; nearly five whole days, in fact. Even so, she'd been hoping that she'd be able to maneuver her into trying to wriggle her way out of getting her tail toasted if she brought it up where lots of people would be able to hear her talking about it, and she was thrilled that she'd been so obliging. She'd spotted an arcade cabinet out of the corner of her eye when they'd first done their initial tour of the place after arriving, and the sight of it had planted the seed of an idea in the back of her mind. Now it had sprouted, and was about to bear fruit.

"I'll tell you what, cutie pie," she began, letting her voice slide into that deceptively casual nonchalance she used whenever she was about to spring something extra mean on her girlfriend that she knew they'd both enjoy. "You're *definitely* going to get a spanking when I get you home, there's no way I'm changing my mind about that. But… in the interest of giving you a fighting chance to not spend all day tomorrow looking for excuses to avoid sitting down, we'll make a game out of it."

Hooking a thumb over her shoulder toward a quiet and lonely corner of the arcade deep in the warren of 90s era beat-em-ups and fighting games, she let a confident smirk quirk up one corner of her mouth. "There's a Mortal Kombat 2 machine over there, and you and I are going to play it. Every match we'll wager something about your spanking. If I win, it happens, but if you win, it doesn't. Sound fair?"

Sensing that she'd just been maneuvered into a trap, but not seeing any way to back out gracefully now, Cassidy did her best to ignore the butterflies performing aerial acrobatics inside her stomach.

"Um… okay. You're on!"

After filling a disposable plastic cup with tokens from a change machine beside the bar, all the other games they'd played up until then had used a more modern card reader system for charging their players, the two of them retired to their dusty little corner of the arcade and squared up in front of the Mortal Kombat machine they found there.

"Alright, for the first match we'll keep things simple," said Lauren, feeding tokens into the machine while Cassidy stood by nervously flexing her fingers and popping her knuckles. "If I win, your panties are coming off. If you win, they stay up. How's that sound?"

"Works for me," replied Cassidy, rolling her shoulders to loosen up as a fresh surge of hope welled up inside of her.

She'd kicked Lauren's ass at Street Fighter not more than half an hour earlier, surely she'd be able to hold her own at this game too. Of course, she hadn't actually *touched* a Mortal Kombat machine in well over a decade and a half, but that should hardly matter... right? "Get ready to lose, bossy boots."

Unfortunately for her, Cassidy soon realized that while Lauren may have sucked at Street Fighter, she was no slouch when it came to Mortal Kombat.

"My mom used to drag me and my brother with her to the bowling alley every Wednesday for league night," she explained, smiling smugly to herself as she finished royally trouncing her girlfriend. "She'd give us each a five, and we'd kill time in the little arcade they had there while she and her friends bowled. They didn't have much, but they *did* have an MK-two machine."

"You know, you could have mentioned that earlier," grumbled Cassidy, still reeling from how quickly the two rounds she'd just played had gone. Lauren had been absolutely ruthless with her. She hadn't stood a chance.

"And you could have asked," countered Lauren with a smirk. "Now I do believe I will be taking those panties of yours, cutie pie. Go on, take em' off, we don't have all night you know."

She turned to face her girlfriend and held out her hand, palm up, crooking her fingers expectantly.

"What?" moaned Cassidy, her hands flying back to the seat of her skirt as if to protect what lay hidden beneath its woolen pleats. "But you said that was for later!"

"I do believe my exact words were, 'If I win, your panties are coming off'. I never said specifically *when* that would be.

You know you really ought to clarify things before you make a bet, hon," taunted Lauren, her smirk turning into something decidedly more predatory as she loomed over Cassidy. "Now are you going to be a good girl and pay up? Or do I need to do it for you?"

Lauren made no move toward Cassidy other than to waggle her fingers at her in mock-impatience, but the gleam in her eye made it perfectly clear that she had zero qualms about shoving her over the front of their arcade cabinet and baring her butt right then and there if she didn't make up her mind soon. Trying to put at least a semi-positive spin on things, Cassidy found herself reasoning that at least if she were the one to take off her panties, there wouldn't be any chance of her skirt "accidentally" being flipped up in the process.

"Ugh, *fine*," she huffed.

Pouting just as hard as she could muster, she cast a quick peek around to make sure that nobody was looking their way just then. Then, with an overwrought sigh she bent her knees slightly and leaned forward, slipping her hands beneath her skirt. Doing her best to keep her movements smooth and inconspicuous, she gripped either side of the elastic waistband of her panties, and with a low whine of mortification, pushed them off of her hips and halfway down her thighs. Gravity mercifully took over from there, and as she straightened up, the loose material slipped down past her knees to pool around her ankles. Blushing scarlet, Cassidy rested one palm on the cabinet in front of her for support, and did her best to untangle her panties from around her high-tops as quickly as possible. This proved to be a bit more difficult than she'd originally anticipated however, but three quick hops, and one near fall to the ground that was only prevented by a timely hand from

Lauren flying out to grab her butt, later, she had the warm fabric of her seafoam-green panties balled up tight in her fist. Now blushing scarlet, Cassidy fixed her girlfriend with an even harder pout, and then deposited them into Lauren's waiting palm.

"Thank you very much, cutie pie," she crooned, stretching her prize between her hands and admiring it thoughtfully for several excruciatingly humiliating seconds before folding it into a neat little rectangle and setting it carefully next to their cup of tokens in front of the arcade cabinet's video display. She gave her girlfriend's forfeited panties a loving pat, and then fished out four more tokens for them. "Now then, I think for this next match we ought to decide just what it is I'll be using to tan that cute little *bare* caboose of yours with."

Four more very one-sided matches Later, Cassidy's thighs were squirming and her heart was racing as Lauren laid out the final results of their "little wagers".

"Let's see," she said as she finished typing the last few details into her phone so she wouldn't forget. "When we get home, you're going to get a spanking with... my belt, and my hand of course. For as long as I want, and... as hard as I want, while... bent over the back of the couch. Oh, and of course we can't forget that after I've finished painting your back porch red, and believe me, it's going to be very red, you're going to spend... fifteen minutes standing in the corner. Oh boy, now doesn't that sound like just so much *fun*, Cassie?"

Truth be told, it actually did sound like a lot of fun to Cassidy, but the cool fingers of the air conditioned breezes circulating through the arcade that had been tickling her between the thighs for the last fifteen minutes as her naked cheeks shifted nervously beneath the pleats of her suddenly much too short feeling skirt, were tempering her anticipation with a healthy amount of dread. She definitely wouldn't be having any fun sitting for her lectures tomorrow, that was for sure. Why couldn't the university invest in some chairs with actual padding? Geez.

Swallowing hard, she managed to flash her girlfriend a wry grin. "I've heard of being a sore loser before, but this is kind of ridiculous, don't you think?"

That made Lauren laugh harder than she'd expected, and even earned Cassidy an affectionate pat to the back of her skirt for her trouble.

"Tell you what," she offered, keeping her hand on Cassidy's tush and fiddling with one of her pleats. "If you want, we can play one more match for double or nothing. If you win, no big spanking, but I'm still keeping your panties. But if I win…"

She paused to let the tension build, slipping her hand beneath the other girl's skirt and giving her right cheek a meaningful squeeze.

"If I win, you and I are going to take a little trip into that party room over there."

She nodded to her left in the direction of a private room meant for kids to gather for cake and ice cream during birthday parties. The door was ajar and the lights were on, but nobody had been in or out of it since they'd started playing.

"And do what?" asked Cassidy, not quite able to keep the tremor of morbidly-curious excitement from her voice as Lauren lightly raked her nails across her ticklish cheeks.

"That's a surprise," cooed Lauren in a singsong voice, letting her fingertips slip tantalizingly close to between Cassidy's thighs. "Are you in?"

Wriggling in place, trying, and failing, to organize her thoughts into something coherent, Cassidy wilted under her girlfriend's commanding touch and agreed to play one last match for double or nothing. Which she then lost handily, Lauren taking two Perfect KO rounds in a row off of her without even breaking a sweat.

"Alright, cutie pie, come with me," she ordered as soon as their match was over, taking Cassidy by the hand and dragging her off toward the private party room to their left before her character had even finished his victory animation, leaving behind their cup of tokens and Cassidy's panties out on top of the machine without a second glance.

Lauren wove her way around a few scattered chairs and discarded party hats, guiding her girlfriend toward the back of the room where she then casually pushed her over the edge of one of the long plastic tables that ran its length. Moving in no particular rush now, she lifted the back of her skirt, exposing her bare cheeks to the extra-chilly air that hung thick in the empty room, as she took her time to carefully roll up her pleats and tuck them into the back of her waistband to ensure that her skirt wouldn't inadvertently fall back down into place before she was finished with her. This little precaution hadn't been lost on Cassidy, but there was nothing she could do about it she knew, and so she just groaned softly and made peace with the fact that if someone were to walk in on them, she would have to be *very* careful to avoid giving them an eyeful of her round and bouncy cheeks.

Speaking of her cheeks, Cassidy was more than a little surprised when no spanks started to rain down against them. Lauren instead just left her bent over and resting on her elbows, staring at the plain-white tabletop stretched out before her as she listened to her fish around for something inside her purse. Assuming that she was looking for a hair-brush or something else to swat her with, she'd been there when Lauren had bought the biggest, heaviest hairbrush she could find to carry with her in her purse "just in case", Cassidy closed her eyes and tried not to think too hard about what might happen if someone got curious about the noises that would soon be coming from their little party room.

"Ah!" gasped Cassidy as she reflexively tried to stand up, only to be pushed roughly back down by Lauren, as she felt something ice cold and wet start to dribble down between her cheeks.

"I've got a surprise for you, Cassie," sang Lauren, using the fingers of her left hand to spread her girlfriend's cheeks wide apart so the icy liquid could more easily trickle down between them.

"Y-You do?" squeaked Cassidy, her face glowing crimson as her mind frantically raced to try and piece together what was happening.

"Tada!" Letting go of her lover's cheeks, Lauren picked up something from the table and brought it around so that it was only a few inches away from Cassidy's grimacing face. That something turned out to be a brand new, matte black, silicone butt plug. "Happy four week anniversary, hon."

"Wha-?" Cassidy's eyes had grown as wide as saucers at the sight of the plug, while her cheeks clenched and unclenched several times as if trying to imagine what it might feel like to have it thrust snugly between them.

The toy in Lauren's hand looked to be nearly five inches long and was tapered to a rounded point on one end before gradually flaring out to over an inch and a half wide near the bottom. From there it flared back in to form a thin spiraled neck that was attached to a perpendicular base that would prevent it from sliding in too deep. All in all it was a very impressive looking butt plug, not that Cassidy had ever actually seen one in person before, and had probably cost her girlfriend a pretty penny. Honestly, she was touched by the gesture and the fact that Lauren had even remembered something silly like their four week anniversary. She was also more than a little aroused at the thought of such a special gift, something that very clearly made the statement "I'm in charge here, and your butt belongs to me". It was the perfect thing to commemorate their budding relationship, and as she got an up close up look at it, Cassidy found herself feeling rather intimidated.

Swallowing a lump in her throat that wasn't entirely to blame on to the sudden influx of butterflies swirling around inside her stomach, she asked. "Um… i-is that going inside of me?"

It was a silly question to ask she knew, but at that moment it was the only thing she could think of to say.

"It sure is," confirmed Lauren, patting her head affectionately. She knew that given the circumstances she wasn't going to get a proper "thank you" from Cassidy quite yet, but she didn't mind. "And since you're being such a good girl, I'll even let you lube it up for me. Say 'ahhhh'."

"Wait, wha-?"

Cassidy's question was cut off mid-sentence as her girlfriend gently, but firmly, took advantage of her confusion to shove her brand new toy in between her parted lips.

"Get it nice and wet for me," she ordered, dragging her

words out melodiously as she carefully turned the plug left, and then right, over and over again. "They only gave us a teeny tiny sample of lube, and I already used all of it up on you just now. So unless you'd like this thing to go in dry, I'd put my back into it, cutie pie."

That certainly provided more than enough motivation for Cassidy, and she spent what she suspected was probably much longer than was really necessary coating her new present in as much saliva as she could. Running her tongue up and down its length as Lauren insistently slid it in and out of her mouth, smiling all the while as she did so and occasionally making snide observations about how big or long her present was.

"There we go," she cooed, eventually plucking the plug from between her girlfriend's lips with an audible "pop" and smirking as a line of spittle clung to its tip from an anchor point on her pouting lower lip. "Now then, if you would be so kind as to reach back and spread those lovely little cheeks of yours for me, we can get this little guy in and move on with our night."

"I r-really wouldn't c-call it 'little'…" gasped Cassidy, her hands pawing desperately at her cheeks to spread them as wide as she could. To her utter humiliation, she found herself unable to resist grinding against the hard edge of the table beneath her as Lauren teased at her back door with the tip of her plug.

"Mmmhmmm?" chuckled Lauren, only half-listening. "Is that so?"

Lauren spent what felt like a very long time easing her plug in, only to ease it right back out again as soon as she'd made any progress. Driving Cassidy up the wall with a whole host of new sensations, she took her time working it deeper and deeper into her, stretching the poor girl's anus a little wider with each new thrust, but never quite seeming to fully push it home. It was an agonizingly slow and blissful torture for her, and just as Cassidy felt like she was about to climax, Lauren shoved the plug roughly into her, rocking her up onto her tip-toes and forcing her to clamp both hands over her mouth to keep from squealing out loud.

POP! POP! POP! POP!

Laruen's palm bounced four times in quick succession against Cassidy's naked cheeks, making them jiggle and bounce before she plopped back down onto her heels with a ragged gasp. She then deftly untucked the back of her skirt from her waistband and smoothed it down across her still wriggling hips. She gave her wrinkled pleats a few cursory brushes with her fingertips to get rid of any clinging bits of lint, and then patted her right between her cheeks where her new toy lay nestled.

"Up and at em', cutie pie," she ordered, helping Cassidy back up onto a pair of wobbly legs. Not giving her any time to recover her wits, she then threaded her right arm through her girlfriend's left and steered her out of the party room, flicking the lights off behind them as they left, chuckling darkly all the while. "You and I have some rematches to take care of first before we go home. I can't *wait* to see how long you hold onto first place when *you're* the one driving around with something shoved up your tail pipe."

Chapter 5

Dinner and a Show

Like just about any other couple, Cassidy and Lauren spent quite a few date nights going to the movies. Most of the time they'd usually just see a re-screening of an older classic at the local discount theater near their campus. The floors may have been sticky, and the screens were way too small, but it was at least well within their price range, and the auditoriums were dark enough to cuddle up in and sneak a quick smooch without attracting dirty looks. Even so, neither of them could resist the siren song of a brand new release for long, and about once every month or so they'd splurge and pay full price to go see something that had just come out at the high-end megaplex just across the street from the mall. It might have cost an arm and a leg, but it was almost always worth it. Almost.

"Good god, that was *such* a piece of shit," grumbled Lauren, pausing just outside the door to their auditorium to toss out the remains of the bucket of popcorn and extra-large Diet Coke they'd been sharing into the chrome garbage can she found there.

"What did you expect?" laughed Cassidy, decidedly less grumpy than her girlfriend was as she slipped past her. "It was a slasher movie about sentient killer cellphones released in the middle of April. Of course it was going to be a dumpster fire."

"That doesn't give them a free pass to be *that* terrible, though," countered Lauren, shuddering theatrically and demonstrating more acting talent than the combined cast of the movie they'd just walked out of. "I mean my god. You could actually *see* the strings holding up the phones as they chased after people in half the scenes. I can't believe we actually paid good money to see that crap."

"Oh come on, it wasn't the worst thing ever," protested Cassidy, pouting just a little. "I thought the kills were pretty cool at least."

"Hah! And how would you know?" smirked Lauren. "As far as I could tell, you were too busy covering your eyes to actually see any of them."

"I was not!" Cassidy did her best to sound indignant, but the twin spots of color that appeared in the centers of either cheek as she said it gave away her fib. "I'll have you know that I was peeking between my fingers for all of the important parts... sort of."

"Sure you were," crooned Lauren, rolling her eyes condescendingly as she dragged out the words with sardonic amusement. "Oh, and don't think for a second that I've forgotten about our little deal, cutie pie."

"Oh come on, Lauren. It wasn't *that* bad!" protested Cassidy, feeling her stomach tighten nervously, as the blush in her cheeks deepened several shades of pink. "We sat through the whole thing, didn't we? That has to count for something, right?"

"Uh-uh." Lauren cut her off with a waggle of her right index finger, still smirking. "I just subjected myself to nearly two hours of what you yourself literally, just now, called a dumpster fire. The plot made no sense, the characters couldn't act to save their lives, and the special effects were atrocious. Which means I was right about it being a total waste of our time and money, and now you're going to pay for it, missy."

"Okay fine, you've got me there I guess," conceded Cassidy, tossing her hands into the air and rolling her own eyes skyward. Of course her words were being used against her. She really should have thought a bit harder before she'd spoken so candidly. Sure the movie had been awful, but it hadn't been, like, *that* awful. Had it? "Can't we just say it was so bad it was actually good?"

"Hah, nice try," snorted Lauren. "But being ironically good doesn't count, I'm afraid."

"Somehow I thought you might see it that way," muttered Cassidy, crossing her arms beneath her chest with a huff.

"Aaaw, you're just so *cute* when you pout," cooed Lauren, sweeping her girlfriend up into a tight embrace and planting a kiss right on her forehead. She then let her hands glide down along the soft material of the navy-blue, fleece dress she was wearing, making her shiver as she raked her nails across her back before gathering up a handful of cheek in each of her palms as they reached her hips. Squeezing hard, she pulled her in close against her as her voice dipped down into a low, sultry purr. "But I bet you'll look even cuter when you're bent over with your panties around your knees and begging me to stop."

Swallowing hard, Cassidy looked shyly up at Lauren as the warm and familiar sensation of looming dread stirred to life inside her lower abdomen, making her knees rub together as it settled down heavily between her thighs.

"But... but won't somebody hear us?" she protested, unable to bring herself to accept her defeat gracefully. Hope sprang eternal after all.

"Maybe." Lauren shrugged, making it all too clear that it

didn't particularly bother her one way or the other if some-one did. She could practically feel the heat radiating up at her from just a few inches below her chin, and that combined with the faint scent of strawberry shampoo tickling her nose was making her all the more eager to make her girlfriend squirm. Tearing her gaze away from the most hypnotic pair of green eyes she'd ever seen, she tilted her head to look past the curly blonde tresses obscuring her line of sight. "It looks like we've got about maybe ten minutes before the other movies start to get out, so I'm sure it'll be fine if we hurry."

The smirk she leveled at Cassidy as she said it however let her know that she didn't care if her math was off.

"Either way, I wouldn't drag my feet unless you'd like an audience for a little 'public screening' of your own, cutie pie," she laughed, letting her gaze slip past Cassidy again, double checking just when it was the other movies were scheduled to end. "Then again, that actually might be fun…"

"No, no, no, that *won't* be necessary!" Cassidy hastened to stomp out that idea before it could fully take root, playfully clamping a hand over her girlfriend's mouth as if she could somehow prevent the words from getting out and becoming actions. She couldn't tell if Lauren was actually being serious or not, and that thought alone sent a cold shiver down her spine. It was embarrassing enough already that she'd allowed herself to be coerced into agreeing to let Lauren give her a spanking if "One Missed Phone Kill" ended up being as ter-rible as the critics had said it was. She didn't need the added humiliation of a bunch of random strangers watching from the sidelines and making snide comments as she was taken to task for her daring taste in cinema.

"Just be glad I didn't put you over my knee right as the

credits started rolling," laughed Lauren, shaking off Cassidy's hand and squeezing her tush a little harder, just to remind her who was in charge in their relationship. "I thought about it you know. That movie was *such* a train wreck."

"Whatever," huffed Cassidy, accepting her fate with a fresh pout to hide the worried giggle that was lurking just beneath the surface. "I still liked it. Now are we going to do this or not?"

Her bravado was paper thin, and they both knew it, but she couldn't help herself. Whenever she got nervous, especially before a spanking, she got talkative. And to make matters worse, she'd found she had a natural talent for being a smart-aleck. It was a dangerous combination to be sure.

"Careful, cutie pie," warned Lauren, releasing her grip on the other girl's rear end and taking a step back. She allowed a dangerous smile to pull at the corners of her lips, turning the look she leveled at her into something feral and predatory. "I'm sure that the liquid soap they've got here works just as well as a bar of Ivory for washing out a sassy mouth."

"I'll be good!"

Cassidy had only ever had her mouth washed out once before, so she wasn't really sure just how viable Lauren's threat was, but she was willing to take her word on the matter for the time being. At least for now at any rate. Her mother had introduced her to the punishment just last Christmas when she'd gotten a bit too mouthy with her, and she could *still* taste the bitter suds on her tongue if she let her mind wander back to that night.

"We'll see."

Chuckling darkly to herself at the abject look of horror that had burst from beneath the cracks in her girlfriend's mask of impudence, Lauren took her hand in hers, turned, and began dragging her off in the direction of the public restrooms near the back of the theater that they'd scouted out earlier before buying snacks.

The inside of the restroom was clean and well-lit by tastefully arranged fluorescent bulbs shining through diffusers above the sink that bathed the slate gray walls in a soft white glow that was easy on the eyes. Just as Lauren had predicted, they were the only two in there at the moment. Everyone else was still glued to their seats while their movies finished their final acts, but that was little comfort to Cassidy who knew that anybody could decide to duck out early if they'd drank too much soda.

"Okey doke, bend over," ordered Lauren cheerfully, guiding her girlfriend over to stand in front of a spot between two of the sinks directly facing the door they'd just come through.

"What?" whined Cassidy, trying not to meet the other girl's eyes through their reflection in the mirror in front of them. "Can't we at least go into one of the stalls or something?"

"Nope." Lauren shrugged again and flashed an unrepentant smirk into the mirror. That had actually been her original plan as she'd led the way toward the restroom, but the sight of the empty counter space in front of them as they'd walked in and its promise to totally mortify her girlfriend had been too great an opportunity to ignore. "Now bend."

She gave Cassidy a firm push between the shoulder blades, and the girl reluctantly tipped forward onto her elbows, her feet automatically stepping a shoulder's width apart to better support her as she arched her back and pushed her round rump out for easy access. She'd gotten a lot of practice bending over things in the last three months, and knew just how to get comfortable right before her butt caught on fire.

"That's my good girl," cooed Lauren, who thankfully didn't drag out the process of raising the back of her dress up to expose the black tights she had on underneath for long, instead just giving it a quick flip up over her hips. She did however pause for a moment to give the snug material of her leggings a couple of appreciative pats, admiring the way they seemed to mold themselves around her ample cheeks, before slipping her fingers into the waistbands of both her panties and her leggings, and tugging them both down at the same time to her knees with practiced ease.

"Say cheese," she teased after taking three steps back and leveling the camera on her phone at her fully-exposed rear end, perfectly framed by the dark tights bunched around her knees and the navy-blue folds of her dress at the small of her back. "Sorry hon, but you're just way too cute *not* to take a before and after shot of I'm afraid."

"Whatever," came Cassidy's half-laugh, half-groan, of a reply as she pushed her caboose out a bit further so it would look its best.

She felt her face flush hot pink and she pouted as hard as she could at her girlfriend's reflection as she photographed her humiliation, secretly hoping her expression would be visible from the angle she was taking her picture from. She knew she had a cute butt, and she definitely enjoyed ogling it in the mirror after a session across Lauren's knee, so she couldn't really bring herself to be too upset with this impromptu photo session.

"Anytime you're ready, maestro," she teased, waggling her bare bottom suggestively behind her and rolling her eyes.

"Of course," apologized Lauren, not actually sounding

sorry in the slightest as she advanced on her girlfriend with a wolfish grin. Sliding in beside her, leaning her left hip against the counter for support, she set a timer on her phone for ten minutes, and then slipped it into her front pocket. "Hang on tight, cutie pie, I've got a *lot* of pent up frustration from that shitty movie to get out of my system."

SMACK! SMACK!

She let fly with two lightning fast, open-palm slaps to the undersides of Cassidy's cheeks, making them bounce as she got a feel for her aim. She quickly built up steam, slapping hard and fast in a random pattern that kept the other girl on her toes both literally and figuratively as she tried to guess where the next swat would land. Sometimes it was a thigh, sometimes a cheek, other times a sit-spot. Lauren didn't think ahead, but just let her body move of its own accord, spanking wherever felt right with varying degrees of speed as she waited for her phone to buzz in her pocket, letting her know it was time to stop.

The individual spanks themselves weren't particularly terrible, each only stinging for a second or two, but Lauren's pace was a distressing combination of lightning-fast and unpredictably erratic, which left her girlfriend with virtually no time to actually catch her breath and get a grip on the heat that was rapidly being fanned into an inferno in her cheeks and thighs. Cassidy for her part, frantically shuffled her weight from foot to foot as Lauren's iron-hard palm rocked her against the edge of the countertop with every swat, the warmth in her bottom gradually starting to dribble down between her thighs as the minutes ticked by with agonizing slowness.

After what felt like an eternity, Lauren's pace slowed and then stopped, and Cassidy was left panting while supporting herself on a pair of wobbly knees. She watched the mirror in front of her through watery eyes as her girlfriend took a few steps back once again and took several more pictures of her handiwork.

"I think you'll be pleased to know that your ass is an absolutely lovely shade of red carpet red right now, Cassie."

Cassidy couldn't really think of anything to say to that just then, and instead let the blush on her upper cheeks that was competing with the one in her lower ones speak for itself as Lauren swept back over to her and busied herself with pulling her panties and leggings back up into place, trapping the blazing inferno in her bottom and thighs beneath them where it would continue to smolder for hours. That done, she gave her tush an affectionate couple of pats before casually tugging her dress back down over her hips, and not a moment too soon as it turned out. It seemed that Lauren had no sooner finished smoothing the material down along her girlfriend's generous glutes, than the door to the restroom had burst open and three eagerly chatting friends had strolled in. They'd all given Cassidy a confused look as they'd caught sight of her still bent over and resting her elbows on the counter in front of her, but Lauren was able to sweep aside their concerns by nonchalantly explaining that she'd dropped a contact lens.

That seemed to satisfy them, even though Cassidy was actually wearing her glasses, and it appeared that nobody was the wiser to what had just been happening only a few moments earlier as they threaded their way through the press of people making their way toward the bathroom. However, as they were nearing the edge of the crowd, they couldn't help overhearing several snippets of conversations.

"Man, what was up with that final scene? Who the heck

thought it was a good idea to randomly toss in a drum track in the middle of a wedding?"

"I know right?"

"It must've been some avant-garde art house thing."

"I guess… that would definitely explain those random yelping sounds too."

"Oh yeah, totally! My brother told me that the director used to do a lot of indie stuff, so I'm sure that's why it was like that."

Lost in their conversation, none of the people they passed noticed either of the two women passing them by, one grinning triumphantly, and the other blushing red as a tomato.

"God, I love the movies."

Chapter 6

Lines in the Library

As the spring semester of her junior year started to draw to a close, Lauren Delaney found herself spending more and more of her time behind a research desk at the university's student library. While the laptop she'd bought the year before was more than up to the task of writing papers and preparing presentations for group projects, she found that she just focused better when she was fully immersed in the subdued ambience of the underground archives in the middle of campus, away from the temptation to "multitask" while working that typically took the form of binging episodes of The Simpsons on Netflix in the background. Whenever she had a major assignment to work on, she'd sequester herself away behind one of the many public computers in the main study area for two or three hours at a time and dedicate herself entirely to the subject at hand. It was a good system for her, and ever since she'd fully embraced it there'd been a noticeable upswing in her grades, and ironically she'd also found herself with a lot more free time to spend with Cassidy since she was able to focus to the point of radically increasing her productivity.

At least, that was how things *usually* went.

One particular afternoon Cassidy had decided to tag along with her after she'd finished her classes for the day, but unfortunately for the both of them, the serene atmosphere of the library didn't seem to have quite the same calming effect on her as it did for Lauren. In fact, it had quite the opposite, magnifying her boredom tenfold as she bounced her attention restlessly from the study guide she'd printed out for her physics final, to her phone where she'd play a few rounds of the one puzzle game she had downloaded that didn't require an active internet connection to work (reception was terrible in the building), to sporadically looking for something interesting to occupy her mind on the highly-restrictive web browser her workstation had installed on it. None of it was able to hold her focus for long however, and as the minutes ticked by at a maddeningly slow crawl, she found herself squirming in her chair and looking for excuses to bug Lauren if for no other reason than to just have something to do.

"Do you think they keep it so cold in here because it helps preserve the books, or is it just because we're underground and it's naturally cold?"

Heaving out an annoyed sigh, Lauren turned away from the monitor of her workstation and fixed the girl next to her with a disapproving scowl.

"Do I need to spank you, Cassie?"

"Oh my god, shhh!"

Cassidy's face had predictably flushed a positively adorable shade of hot pink as she'd scrambled to hush the other girl up with a frantic waving motion. She swallowed her embarrassment and cast a nervous glance to either side behind her, trying to see if anybody had overheard what she'd just been asked. It was hard to say for certain, there were quite a few people using computers around them, but none of them were looking in her direction at least. Still though, she kept her voice barely above a whisper, hoping that Lauren would do the same, as she hissed.

"And no, you *don't*. Thank you very much."

She huffed, blowing several loose strands of hair out of her face and folding her arms under her chest as she slouched in her chair and glared with embarrassment at her computer monitor and the scary story about a haunted video game cartridge that she'd only been half-reading while Lauren had typed away at one of her term papers next to her. Sitting around trying to kill time in the library was proving to be way more boring than she'd originally bargained for, but as much as she would have loved to have been at home in her pajamas doing *anything* else just then, Lauren had been the one to give her a ride onto campus that morning and it was raining way, way too hard for her to try and walk the mile and a half back home to their apartment. So she was effectively stranded on campus until Lauren decided she'd done enough studying for one evening, whenever the heck that would that would be.

Seeing that she'd cowed Cassidy, at least for the moment, Lauren let a satisfied smirk play across her angular features as she directed her attention back to her work. This time her girlfriend's focus lasted for an entire, blissfully silent, ten minutes before it finally slipped again and she started pestering her about how much longer she planned on staying there for and whether or not she thought the library's vending machines might take her student ID card as a form of payment, and if they even had the candies she liked in them.

"Not that I'm really in the mood for candy," mused Cassidy to herself. "Honestly, I'd much rather have something warm right now. Do you think they have a microwave around here I could borrow? I think some of the vending machines in Beckler Hall sell Hot Pockets, so I could maybe get one of those and bring it here..."

Pinching the bridge of her nose and sighing again, Lauren marked her place in the book she'd been using as reference material, saved her progress on her paper, and locked her workstation. Gathering up her purse, she pushed her chair back from the desk and stood. She then rounded on her girl-friend, fuming silently, and cut off her stream of consciousness chit-chat with a surprised squeak as she snatched her upper arm up in an iron grip and began dragging her off deeper into the bowels of the library.

"Wait, Lauren, wait!" protested Cassidy with strained panic, not wanting to draw any attention to either of them if she could avoid it as she was frog-marched down a flight of stairs and into one of the more seldom-trafficked sections of the library. "I promise I'll be good, just give me another chance, please!"

"Uh-uh," answered Lauren sharply, giving her girlfriend's upper-arm a hard squeeze as she suddenly veered off down a hall to their right and swept her into one of the four mini con-ference rooms that took up a large portion of the sub-base-ment, letting the door slam shut behind them. "You've been begging for this ever since you got here, cutie pie, and I'm not letting you off the hook without giving you exactly what you've earned."

Her initial blood-boiling annoyance had dissipated by the time she'd escorted the two of them into this private little meeting room, having been replaced by the usual electric tin-gles of excitement she always felt whenever she was about to do something mean to her girlfriend. She was still determined to tear up Cassidy's bratty little butt for being such a pest. They both knew she needed it if for no other reason than to provide her with an outlet for all of her pent up restlessness, but her plans were no longer purely rooted in the realm of disciplinary punishment. After all, Lauren reasoned to herself as she let go of her girlfriend's arm and cast an appraising look around the room she'd picked more or less at random, if she was going to take the time out of her busy study schedule to correct Cassidy's bad behavior, the least she could do was make it something fun and memorable.

That's when she spotted the long, thin, and very *mean* looking wooden cane lying innocently on top of the conference table. Well, technically it was a pointer stick, not an actual cane like the ones she'd read about in some of the stories Cassidy had shared with her on her Kindle not too long after they'd started dating, but it was close enough for what she had in mind just then. It was about half an inch thick and as long as her arm, made from some sort of tan colored wood and capped on either end with red rubber tips. Snatching it up from the table, Lauren gave it an experimental flex in her hands, finding to her delight that it was surprisingly springy, and then slashed it through the air beside her.

SWISH SWISH

The long, thin, makeshift cane whizzed through the air with almost no resistance, cutting through it with a satisfyingly intimidating "whoosh" sound that split Lauren's features into a wide, feral grin. An impromptu idea for just how to play this little scene of theirs out had started to form in the back of her mind when she'd noticed the pointer on the table, and now as she flexed it between her hands, taking in the sight of Cassidy nervously chewing at her thumbnail as she stared transfixed at the center of her chest, she knew just what she wanted to do.

"Well, Cassie," she began, making her voice stern and clinical as she directed a disapproving scowl down her nose in the other girl's direction. "Since you seem so dead set on acting like a naughty little schoolgirl, I think it's only appropriate that I treat you like a naughty little schoolgirl."

"Eep," squeaked Cassidy, half in jest and half out of a need to *do anything just* then that might help quell some of the butterflies roiling around inside her stomach.

"Eep indeed," replied Lauren with a wink, her stern headmistress mask slipping just a bit beneath the weight of her amusement. "Now as to your punishment, I think that, oh... let's say six... no, better make it *twelve* of the very best with the cane on your bare bottom ought to be enough to instill some measure of proper discipline in you, at least until 'study hall' has finished."

Cassidy felt her shoulders sag a bit with relief as she heard this pronouncement. Sure, that stick in Lauren's hands looked like it could really pack a wallop, but she knew she could handle twelve. She'd taken a whole heck of a lot more than that from her girlfriend's belt only a few days earlier, and the couple of times her mom had taken a switch to her when she'd been younger had lasted *way* longer than that as well. She was confident that she'd be able to take whatever Lauren decided to dish out with at least some modicum of grace. She'd definitely be sore by the time she was finished with her if the stories she'd read about British-style school canings were anything to go by, but honestly, how bad could it really be?

Something of her relief must have shown on her face, because Lauren's brows quickly knitted together into a glower.

"I see that you find something amusing about that," she observed darkly, embracing her grumpy headmistress role all the more as she tipped Cassidy's chin up with the end of her cane so she could bring the full weight of her steely glare to bear on her. "Very well then, young lady, have it your way. We shall make it *three* dozen with the cane instead. That ought to be enough to wipe that impudent smirk off your face you... you rapscallion!"

It was. The bemused smirk on Cassidy's face at her girl-friend's silly persona had bent into a worried grimace under the weight of fresh anxiousness as her sentence was suddenly tripled, and she found herself swallowing hard.

"I'm sorry, ma'am!" she squeaked, the words tumbling out of her before she'd even realized she was saying them.

"I should hope so," sniffed Lauren, reveling in their impromptu role play session. She gave her cane another vicious slash through the air that filled the heavy silence in the room with a terrifying *SWISH* that made Cassidy's hips jerk forward involuntarily. "Disrupting the study time of your fellow students is totally unacceptable, Miss Coleman, and you will pay for your indiscretion with your bottom, you naughty, *naughty* girl."

Striding past Cassidy with a haughty scowl on her face, she took up a position near the edge of the table that occupied most of one side of the room and turned her back toward it to face the open area of carpet directly in front of the door they'd walked through not more than a minute or two earlier. She flexed her makeshift cane once more between her hands while she took a moment to decide just how best to position Cassidy for her punishment, and then used its tip to point at a square of carpet about two feet in front of her.

"Come here, girl, and assume the position," she ordered sharply, swishing her cane for emphasis. "Legs a shoulder's width apart, and bent over grabbing your ankles. Come now, don't dawdle. We haven't got all day you know."

Cassidy's stomach did several flip-flops as she moved on jelly legs to stand where she'd been directed to. Swallowing hard, she cast a furtive glance over her shoulder to make sure that the blinds on the observation window behind them had at least been drawn down. Unfortunately for her there was nothing she could do about the narrow vertical window that ran the length of the door behind her, and anybody who happened to look through it would be treated to an unobstructed view of her round, jiggly, buns as Lauren painted vivid red stripes across them, so she just did her best to try and put that possibility out of her mind. Hoping desperately that the small amount of soundproofing the conference room's painted cinderblock walls offered would be enough to keep anybody from hearing what was happening and coming to investigate, she let out a nervous breath and bent at the waist, seizing her ankles in a death grip as her long hair cascaded down around her head to obscure her vision.

"Very good," praised Lauren, setting her cane down behind her on the table as she advanced on her jackknifed girlfriend. "It's reassuring to see that you are at least capable of following orders, albeit under the threat of discipline. Hopefully this lesson will help motivate you to be just as obedient in the future without the need for your knickers to come down."

"Yes ma'am," squeaked Cassidy again. She felt silly repeating herself like that, but it seemed the safest option at the moment as she felt the hem of her skirt being lifted up over her hips and folded over to lie across her back.

"Well now," gasped Lauren, pouring as much indignation into the two words as she could muster once she'd revealed the pink and white polka dots of her girlfriend's very flattering panties. "These are *hardly* regulation, now are they, young lady?"

"Um, uh… no ma'am?" Cassidy answered tentatively, not really sure what "regulation" panties were supposed to look like in the school setting they were creating on the fly, but assuming that they probably weren't nearly as colorful or revealing as hers were.

"No indeed," agreed Lauren with a sniff, clucking her tongue as she straightened out a couple of wrinkles in the soft material. "I'm afraid I'm going to have to confiscate these knickers, dear. We simply cannot have our students running around in such… such… *rebellious* underthings."

Cassidy couldn't help snorting at that, and neither could Lauren, though that didn't seem to slow her down much as she hooked her thumbs into the waistband of the offending panties and whisked them down to the other girl's ankles. With a couple of encouraging pats and a firm squeeze or two from her impromptu headmistress, Cassidy managed to awkwardly untangle her faux-leather boots from the leg holes of her panties, and Lauren snatched them up, tucking them away triumphantly into her purse.

"Scandalous, just *scandalous*," she huffed, doing a terrible job of hiding her amusement as she gathered up her pointer stick in her right hand and swished it menacingly just behind Cassidy's now very vulnerable bare bottom. Her girlfriend's cheeks clenched and unclenched reflexively with each bone chilling *SWISH* of the cane as it cut through the air and produced small puffs that tickled their way across her sensitive skin. Watching her squirm and flex her knees nervously, Lauren's urge to make her cry only grew stronger.

"You are to maintain your position and count out each stroke as it is given," she said calmly as she tap, tap, tapped the length of the cane across the centers of her lover's tautly stretched cheeks, getting a feel for her aim as she swung her arm through several slow-motion practice swings. "Failure to do so will result in the stroke not counting. Is that understood?"

"Yes ma'am..."

SWISH-CRACK!

Lauren delivered the first stroke of Cassidy's caning without any warning, snapping the implement down across her cheeks as hard as she felt she safely could without running the risk of drawing blood.

"Aiieee!" Cassidy knees buckled with the force of the impact and she let out a high-pitched squeal of surprise and pain as a tightly focused line of white hot agony erupted across both of her cheeks simultaneously. She hissed sharply through clenched teeth, riding out the pain as it burrowed deep into her, and shook her hips as much as she could while still clinging to her ankles, before straightening her legs back out with a long exhalation. "One ma'am..."

A perfectly straight, fat red welt had risen up to stand in sharp contrast against the pristinely smooth alabaster backdrop of Cassidy's bare bottom where the cane had bitten into her. It was about an inch or so higher than where Lauren had been aiming for, but that didn't bother her too much as she watched it bounce up and down in time with Cassidy's frantic gyrations. It was beautiful and horribly painful looking, and it took a supreme effort of will on her part not to reach out and pinch it ruthlessly.

"Very good."

SWISH-CRACK!

Again another lurid red line burst into existence across Cassidy's wobbling cheeks, about two inches below the first one.

"T-two ma'am!"

Damn. Lauren bit back a curse as she observed her handiwork and readjusted her grip on that cane. She hadn't been aiming *that* low!

SIWSH-CRACK!

"Ah! Owie, owie, owie!" squealed Cassidy, shifting her weight feverishly from foot to foot as a third welt appeared right between the first two. "Oh my god, *three*, ma'am!"

Much better. Lauren felt her smile widen as she took in the sight of the tightly packed three stripes standing out against her girlfriend's bare bottom.

"Oh don't worry, cutie pie," she teased, lining the cane up again for another stroke. "We've only got thirty three more of these to go."

Cassidy just groaned.

Fifteen minutes, and thirty three equally cruel cane strokes later, Cassidy's bottom and most of her thighs were painted with an angry crisscrossing patchwork of swollen, maroon welts. Lauren had eventually ran out of space with about a dozen strokes left in Cassidy's punishment, and had decided to make those last twelve extra awful by layering them diagonally on top of her other stripes, which had been enough to push poor Cassidy over the edge and into tears. But to her credit, she'd managed to stick it out for her entire punishment, thanks in no small part to a little gentle encouragement and light threatening from Lauren, and now stood sniffling and wiping away tears from her eyes with a proud smile on her face.

"You did great, cutie pie," praised Lauren, beaming as she tossed her pointer over her shoulder without looking and swept up behind Cassidy to coo over her handiwork.

"You want a picture?" she asked with a wide grin, fishing her phone from her front pocket and sliding open its camera app from the home screen. "Your marks are totally gorgeous."

"Yes *please*!" laughed Cassidy, bending back over and poking her throbbing, aching backside out behind her with a mock-pout. "I certainly worked hard enough to get them."

"No kidding," agreed Lauren with a chuckle of her own, snapping several photos in a row from different angles before deciding she probably had enough to pick out two or three perfect ones.

All she wanted to do just then was kneel down behind her girlfriend and shove her face between her thighs while she squeezed and pinched her welts mercilessly, but... that would have to wait. She really did still have a term paper to finish, and the sooner she got that knocked out of the way, the sooner she could have fun with Cassidy. Still though, as she idly groped and squeezed the other girl's left cheek while lost in thought, imagining how nice it would be to have her over her knee as she kneaded soothing lotion into her battered buns, an idea occurred to her that was just way too perfect to ignore.

"Stay right there for a sec, cutie pie. I've got an idea for something to help you stay quiet while I finish working."

Cassidy wanted to point out that the tenderness in her flaming behind that she was still trying to come to grips with was probably more than enough to keep her occupied while

Lauren did her homework, but she wisely decided to clamp down on that particular urge as she watched her dig around inside her purse. She was curious to know what Lauren had up her sleeve, but had a sneaking suspicion it would probably be something humiliating that would drive her up the wall while her girlfriend watched on smugly. Her suspicion proved to be an accurate one as she watched on in horror as Lauren retrieved a small bottle of lube from her purse and set it on the conference table, followed a moment later by the big, matte-black silicone butt plug she'd bought for her to celebrate their four week anniversary.

"I've been looking for an excuse to send you to school while plugged for a while now," explained Lauren casually as she dribbled a small amount of lube along the length of the plug, rotating it slowly as she went so that it got an even coat all across its smooth surface. "The thought of you walking around with this little guy nestled between your cheeks all day is just so hot, don't you think?"

Cassidy just gave her girlfriend a bashful grin at that, not wanting to admit out loud that she did indeed think that that sounded *very* fun, all the while knowing that the glistening lips peeking between her slightly parted thighs would speak volumes for her as Lauren advanced on her with plug in hand. She groaned a little and chewed at her lower lip as Lauren used the fingers of her free hand to roughly part her cheeks, and then gasped and squirmed as the wet and icy-cold tip of the plug pushed up insistently against her tightly puckered rosebud.

"Relax…" ordered Lauren gently, but firmly, as she waited for Cassidy to comply before easing the plug into her.

By now Cassidy was used to having her "little friend" as

Lauren liked to call it inserted into her, and she let out a long exhalation as it was pushed deeper and deeper inside of her, stretching her around its girth before coming to a sudden stop as her anus cinched in around its fluted neck. Cassidy took in and released another deep breath, and then braced herself for Lauren to activate the vibrator. She hadn't known that that was a feature of the plug the first time Lauren had put it in her, but it hadn't taken very long into her second time around with it to realize just how much a high-powered vibration motor shoved deep inside her well-spanked bottom could make her squirm. She'd nearly come right as it had kicked on the first time, and she hadn't gotten any better about controlling herself since then. But strangely enough, the vibrations didn't come, and just as Cassidy was resigning herself to her fate with a mixture of disappointment and relief, Lauren spoke.

"I can do a lot more than just control how fast or slow this thing vibrates using that app on my phone, you know," she teased, releasing her girlfriend's wobbly, swollen cheeks and giving their center a loving pat. "There's actually a very special feature your plug has that I think you'll find quite interesting."

Swallowing hard, Cassidy clenched her cheeks around the toy and shuddered.
"Wh-what's that? Ah!"

She got her answer even before she'd finished asking her question, as the plug suddenly started to vibrate in concert with her words as she spoke them, its intensity shifting to match her volume as she went from speaking normally to gasping in surprise.

"Tada," sang Lauren, her words also making the plug rumble for a brief moment inside of her. "In case you haven't quite worked it out yet, cutie pie, I can use the microphone on my phone to control when and how hard your little friend vibrates. So..."

She drew the word out, bringing her phone right up to her mouth and grinning from ear to ear.

"Unless you want to give everyone upstairs a show with those *adorable* little gasps and squeaks of yours, I'd keep my mouth zipped nice and tight."

Cassidy just nodded frantically, but silently.

Unfortunately for her, she forgot to consider the fact that all of the public workstations in the library used mechanical keyboards. Mechanical keyboards that made very loud and very distinct *CLICK-CLACK* noises whenever somebody typed something on them, and Lauren still had a two thousand word research paper to complete.

That evening ended up being the most productive study session Lauren Delaney ever had.

"We really ought to spend more time together at the library, you know, it's just so... peaceful."

Chapter 7

Bargain Buys for Bratty Buns

Spring semester was finally over, and Lauren and Cassidy were both enjoying the three week break they had before their summer semester started up and it was back to the academic grind for the two of them. One lazy Saturday morning, Lauren had decided that it would be a fun to drive out into the suburbs a few miles away from campus and spend some time walking around the local neighborhood park there, soaking up the warmth from the sun before the weather got too hot to be enjoyable and stretching their legs after being cooped up for so long studying. Cassidy had thought the idea had sounded like a great time the night before, but being the night owl that she was, her opinions had shifted dramatically by the time Lauren yanked the covers off of her at half past ten the following morning. She'd whined and complained that it was way too early to be up and doing things, and that she had to stockpile sleep while she still could, but Lauren flipping her onto her stomach and unceremoniously yanking down her pajama bottoms and panties in back for a brisk thirty spanks with her bedside hairbrush proved to be just the motivation she needed for her to change her mind.

After doing two or three circuits around the meandering jogging paths that were woven throughout the sprawling park, Lauren and Cassidy had both had their fill of natural splendor, but weren't quite ready to head home just yet. And so, they found themselves wandering off into the neighborhood at large, admiring the upper middle class homes lining the streets with no particular destination in mind, just enjoying the sights and occasionally making comments here or there about someone's tacky lawn ornaments or stopping to say hello to people out walking their dogs.

"Hey look, a yard sale," said Lauren, pointing a few houses down the street to where a handful of people were milling about around a series of folding tables someone had set up on their driveway. "You want to check it out?"

"Totally," said Cassidy, nodding eagerly. She already had visions of rare finds at bargain basement prices dancing in her head. Surely there'd be some sort of hidden treasure there just waiting to be unearthed by a discerning eye like hers. "Do you think they'll have any games?"

"Maybe," shrugged Lauren, smiling fondly at her girlfriend's enthusiasm and wrapping an arm around her shoulders as she guided the two of them over to the house in question. She herself wasn't really looking for anything in particular, nor did she have a strong desire to paw around through other people's junk, but a little bit of casual looky looing wouldn't hurt.

The selection of things for sale proved to be, not surprisingly to either of them truth be told, rather mundane. The goods on offer consisted mostly of piles and piles of old clothes that were either way too small or way too out of style for either Lauren or Cassidy to ever seriously consider wearing, several CDs with either damaged of missing cases, and a few super obsolete home electronics, along with the usual various other knick knacks and mementos that'd clearly been piling up in the family's closets for years.

Wrinkling her nose at the cloud of dust she'd stirred up while picking her way through a pile of handmade sweaters, Cassidy decided that the yard sale was a total bust and that it was time to leave. Turning to look for Lauren, she was just about to call out to her and suggest that they move on when she spotted her at one of the tables near the front of the garage, cradling something appraisingly in her hands and smirking.

"What'd you find?" she started to ask as she moved to stand beside her, before cutting her words off in a strangled squawk as she got a good look at what had caught the other girl's attention.

"Isn't this just the most beautiful paddle you've ever seen?" asked Lauren, letting her voice carry far enough to draw the attention of the older woman manning the cash box at the other end of the driveway who was currently making change for a beleaguered looking man balancing a stack of VHS tapes in one hand and clutching the hand of a small child with the other.

"Shhh! Keep your voice down!" hissed Cassidy, snatching the paddle away from her snickering girlfriend before she could draw any more attention to the two of them. "And give me that."

Letting out a long-suffering sigh and rolling her eyes, she looked down at the thing in her hands and found herself having to admit that the paddle actually *was* rather impressive. She could feel the tips of her ears burning and her heart pounding hard against her chest as she turned it over in her hands, examining it closely in spite of the fact that it suddenly felt like everybody was staring at her and could read her mind. She wasn't amazing when it came to guessing the size of things, something that Lauren had had no small amount of fun teasing her about when she'd first introduced her to her strap on, but by her estimation she guessed that the paddle was about eighteen inches long and probably a little over half an inch thick, with well rounded edges and no sharp corners. Its handle had been shaped down and out into a sweeping curve at the bottom, almost like a teardrop, and felt surprisingly comfortable to hold onto as she wrapped her fingers around it and gave the paddle an experimental swing through the air, trying to picture what it would feel like impacting with a naughty bottom.

She felt a tingle flutter between her legs, and had to swallow hard.

She had no idea what kind of wood the paddle was made from, but guessed that it had to be something exotic and fancy since it was a very unique shade of reddish-plum and was surprisingly heavy. Cassidy had no doubt that it could make quite the lasting impression with very little effort, and she found herself smiling wistfully. Someone had taken the time to hand-engrave the words "ATTITUDE ADJUSTER" in two neat rows of big, blocky letters that took up almost all of one side of its business end, and had then filled in the grooves with white paint that made the phrase stand out in stark contrast against the dark wood, making it abundantly clear exactly what the implement was intended for. The rest of its surface had also been polished to a mirror finish and felt silky smooth to the touch as she ran her fingertips along it, imagining what it would feel like rubbing in slow circles across her naked cheeks while she lay bent over the back of their couch or on her stomach, propped up by a pile of pillows.

She shivered. Why was she even thinking about something

like that? There was no way she'd ever have the guts to buy something like this at a yard sale of all places... would she?

"You like that, do you?" asked a motherly voice from directly across the table, startling Cassidy and making her drop the paddle in surprise.

"Ah! No, I was just-!"

"Careful, cutie pie," admonished Lauren with a wink, easily snatching the paddle out of the air before it could clatter to the ground and brandishing it at her with a mock-threat. "You break it, you buy it."

"Oh I wouldn't worry about that beauty breaking any time soon," laughed the older woman.

She appeared to be in her mid to late fifties and was the quintessential picture of a "mom" as she stood there smiling pleasantly at the two of them in a billowy pair of black and white horizontal-striped pants and a navy blue boat-neck top. Possibly sniffing out a potential sale, or maybe just being bored with dealing with the thinned out late-morning yard sale crowd, she'd brought her steel cash box with her over to their end of the driveway and had set it on the table before her expectantly.

"I used that paddle to bust the butts of my three kids about once every couple weeks for nearly thirty years before they finally all moved out, and believe you me, if it was going to break, it would have done so *long* before now."

She gave the two of them a wink as she said that, Cassidy's bright red face and Lauren's self-satisfied smirk not going unnoticed by her sharp eyes as laugh lines crinkled at their corners.

"You don't say?" crooned Lauren, dragging out the words

as she turned to leer at Cassidy and whacked the paddle menacingly against her palm. It made a startling loud *POP* noise and she winced at the sudden sting, but it was well worth it for the little involuntary jerk of Cassidy's hips at the sound. Especially when they bumped into the table in front of her, making it rock on its wobbly legs.

"Careful, young lady," warned the older woman sharply, flashing a frosty glare at Cassidy that melted immediately as she turned her attention to Lauren and beamed.

"My husband made that for Annie, our oldest, when she was about... oh nine or ten I think, and as I said, it's seen more than its fair share of action over the years." She paused and sighed, clearly caught up in a wave of nostalgia as her gaze shifted to the paddle and she smiled softly. "I'd planned on holding onto it in case it was ever needed again, or maybe to pass it on to one of my daughters for when they've got kids of their own, but..."

She paused again, this time to shrug and roll her eyes.

"Kids don't seem to be in the cards for any of them anytime soon, and that thing's just been gathering dust on top of the refrigerator for a couple years now. I figured I'd just throw it out onto the pile today with all the other junk and see if anybody wants it. Are you two interested?"

"No!"

Cassidy hastened to assure the woman that they were in fact *not* interested in her paddle, but her protest was overshadowed by Lauren as she grinned from ear to ear.

"Maybe."

This brought a bemused look to the other woman's face, and she chuckled.

"Well?"

She turned her attention entirely to Lauren then, ignoring Cassidy as she glowered petulantly at her as she spoke.

"Doug says that he made that paddle out of rosewood, which I'm led to believe is supposed to be rather expensive, and he *did* work very hard to make it, but... I'd be willing to let it go for... oh I don't know... thirty?"

Lauren smirked. "Fifteen."

"Twenty-five," countered the woman.

"Lauren!" whined Cassidy, actually stomping a foot beside her girlfriend in spite of herself.

"Hush, Cassie," dismissed Lauren with a curt wave of her free hand as she shared a knowing look with the woman across the table from her.

"Yes dear, the adults are talking," added the other woman, winking at Lauren.

Rather than protest any further and give the two of them more fodder to tease her with, Cassidy just folded her arms under her chest and pouted. It was clear to her that the yard sale lady had somehow picked up on the nature of her relationship with Lauren. She couldn't be sure if the woman actually *believed* that Lauren was going to use that wicked looking paddle on her, but she could clearly see that the threat of it alone was enough to make her squirm, which seemed to amuse her greatly.

"Twenty. And that's my final offer," declared Lauren, staring down the older woman with the full force of her confident half-smirk.

"Please say no, please say no, please say no," chanted Cassidy silently to herself, crossing her fingers under her arms and not actually knowing if she wanted the woman to accept the offer or not.

Either way, she let her and Lauren stew for several long moments as she appeared to mull the offer over, before finally shrugging.

"Done."

"Pleasure doing business with you," cooed Lauren as she fished her wallet out of her purse and passed the woman a twenty dollar bill. She then carefully tucked her new paddle into her purse alongside her wallet and keys, only to discover that the bag was too small for it. That didn't seem to bother her much though, and its dark red handle was left sticking out of the top of her purse as she slung it back over her shoulder. "Say thank you, Cassie."

"Thank you, Cassie," grumbled Cassidy peevishly, not able to quite meet the older woman's smiling eyes as Lauren threaded an arm through hers and steered her away from the table and toward the street, back to their car.

"You ladies have a wonderful day," laughed the older woman from behind them as she unlocked her cash box and dropped the twenty into it. "And have fun."

"Oh, I'm *sure* we will," laughed Lauren, throwing one last smirk over her shoulder.

Cassidy's face stayed flushed tomato-red all the way back to Lauren's car.

"I can't believe you actually bought that stupid thing," she grumbled as she threw herself into her seat with a huff and reached over to put on her seat belt. "That was *so* humiliating."

"I know, I know," soothed Lauren gently as she put the

car into gear and started to drive away. "But I saw the way your knees were wobbling when you were looking at it, and I just couldn't resist. You were practically drooling over it you know."

"I was *not!*"

"Were so," teased Lauren. "We could both see how much you wanted it, cutie pie."

"Ugh, whatever," fumed Cassidy, crossing her arms and slouching in her seat with a moody pout.

"Pardon me?" asked Lauren, not turning to look at her girlfriend, but still arching an eyebrow and letting her voice dip into that dangerous nonchalance she knew all too well.

"I *said*," bit out Cassidy, not looking away from her window as she put as much attitude and sass as she could into each word. "What, ever, *Lauren.*"

"That's what I thought," sighed Lauren, shaking her head and smirking.

Five minutes later, they pulled into the parking lot of a small, local grocery store, and parked in a spot near the back.

"What's up?" asked Cassidy, her pouting all but forgotten as she shimmied up from her slouch and turned to face her girlfriend. "Did you want to get something to make for dinner tonight?"

"Hmm, that's not a bad idea," conceded Lauren as she put the car into park and turned off the ignition. Opening her door and gathering up her purse, the paddle's red handle still sticking out of it like a humiliating beacon, she turned in her seat to face Cassidy and flashed her a wolfish grin.

"But first you and I are going to have a little talk about that attitude of yours, cutie pie, and see how well our new paddle works for adjusting it."

Chapter 8

Rest Stops and Attitude Adjustments

The beginning of summer semester was right around the corner, but before classes could start up again next week, Lauren and Cassidy had decided it would be a fun idea to take a little road trip down to visit Cassidy's family to celebrate her birthday together that weekend. Well, to be fair, calling their little trek a "road trip" would have been overstating things just a little bit since it was only about a two hour drive to her parent's house, but they planned on staying there all weekend and driving back Monday morning, so as far as either of them were concerned it was close enough.

"Cassie, if you don't stop messing with the radio and just pick a station, I'm going to pull this car over," warned Lauren, only half-meaning it.

She could tell that the other girl was feeling antsy about their upcoming visit to her parents' house, and not only because she hadn't seen them in person since Christmas break. This weekend was going to be the first time that her mother and father, and her younger sister, were going to get a chance to properly meet the person she'd been dating for so long now. Lauren knew that Cassidy's family was well aware that they were an item by now. There was no way that Cassidy would ever be able to keep something like that to herself for long. She usually called to check in with them about once every other week and would spend close to an hour chit-chatting with her mother and sister, catching each other up on what had been happening in their lives, and as far as she'd been able to tell from the details she'd managed to get out of her (often under the duress of a few sharp swats), they all seemed to be totally fine with having a lesbian in the family. Cassidy had never really given her the impression that either of her parents, or her younger sister for that matter, were particularly backwards thinking when it came to things like that, but it was still reassuring to know that she wouldn't be introducing Lauren as her "special friend" to anybody that weekend.

"Fine, fine, whatever…"

Cassidy eventually settled on a station that played Top 40 hits, and the two of them began to sing along with what was playing before the song came to an end and the broadcast cut to a commercial.

"Ugh, I hate terrestrial radio," she whined. "Why didn't you pack an aux cord or something?"

"I *did* pack an aux cord," corrected Lauren gently. "It's just that our stupid phones are 'too advanced' for head-phone jacks, and neither of us thought to bring an adapter. Remember?"

"Whatever," huffed Cassidy again, pouting more for the sake of it than out of any actual strong feelings on the subject.

She and Lauren had debated the merits of omitting head-phone jacks on smartphones enough times by now to know perfectly well where each of them stood on the issue, and it wasn't worth another round of trying to explain to her that nobody ever used regular headphones anymore since wire-less headsets were so cheap. Besides, the last time she'd tried to extoll the virtues of phasing out obsolete interfaces in the name of progress, she'd wound up spending most of the night sitting on a sore bottom and writing lines (by hand, ugh) while Lauren watched TV next to her and gloated.

Cassidy continued to flip through a few more stations, much to the annoyance of her girlfriend who was happy to just endure a few minutes of inane local advertising rather than keep bouncing around for something new every few seconds, and eventually she settled back on the station she'd started at in the first place just as the commercial break was wrapping up. They listened to three more songs, blessedly without any interruptions save for a station identification, but it was quickly growing more and more apparent that Cassidy was getting bored.

"I hate car trips," she complained to nobody in particular. "Are we there yet?"

"Are you seriously asking me that, *again?*" demanded Lauren, laughing a little in spite of the twinge of annoyance the question brought with it. Cassidy had been asking her the same question, or at least some slight variation of it, off and on ever since they'd started driving. It was cute the first time, but much less so by the third time. She knew she was doing it mostly because it bugged her, but it was really starting to get old now. She motioned in exasperation with her right hand toward the dashboard. "You can see the GPS right there. You *know* we're still about an hour out, so quit asking."

"Or what?" taunted Cassidy with an impish grin. "You'll turn this car around and take us home?"

"No," answered Lauren slowly, letting some of her strained patience leak into her voice as she flicked on her turn signal and wove her way around a car in front of them that was driving ten miles below the speed limit. "But I *will* pull over at the nearest rest top I can find and put you over my knee."

She knew that that sounded like more of an invitation than an actual threat, and truth be told, she was pretty okay with that. She loved it when Cassidy bratted her, especially when she got all bashful and nervous whenever she threatened to do something about it, but she was also getting sick of hearing the same question over and over again. If her girlfriend decided to keep pushing her luck, she was going to find herself paying for it dearly.

"I didn't forget to pack the Attitude Adjuster, you know," added Lauren with a dangerous twitch of her lips. "And I'd be more than happy to put it to work if I think *your* attitude needs some adjusting, cutie pie."

That little revelation made the smirk on Cassidy's face go a bit crooked, but at the same time it did an excellent job of making her lower abdomen clench with a giddy thrill. Getting spanked at a rest stop would definitely be something new and exciting in their little game of cat and mouse, although it would be devastatingly humiliating if Lauren actually decided to make good on her promise. Even if she was fairly certain that she'd park somewhere out of the way and keep the windows rolled up while she had her across her knee in the middle of the back seat, Cassidy still couldn't be sure that someone wouldn't notice what was happening. So far, or at least so far as she was aware at any rate, she'd been fortunate enough to avoid having anybody actually see Lauren spanking her. Or if they had seen her, they hadn't done anything other than smirk to themselves and move on about their business. Either way, the thought of someone else standing by and watching her get spanked like the naughty little brat she so often was made her squirm more than anything else could, except for maybe that darn Attitude Adjuster, and it ended up proving far too great a temptation to resist.

Cassidy kept her mouth shut and pretended to sulk while she let the radio play on through a few more songs, not wanting to seem too obvious about things when she decided to make her next move. She let Lauren think that maybe her threats had properly cowed her enough that she was going to be quiet for the rest of the trip, which honestly wasn't too far off from the truth since the threat of a session with the Attitude Adjuster was enough to make her take pause, all the while biding her time and thinking of just the right sassy remark to use next. Then, just when she thought she might burst from the tension of it all, she struck.

"Lauren," she whined, stretching her girlfriend's name out for several extra syllables as she flopped herself back against her seat in irritation. "How much longer do you think it's going to be? Can't you go any faster? I'm so *bored*!"

She even stamped her feet for good measure, just to be safe. She might've been laying it on a little thick, but she knew how much Lauren loved taking her to task for throwing a tantrum. And apparently that afternoon was no exception.

"Okay then," Lauren sighed heavily, running a hand over her forehead and through her dark hair in exasperation, but also smiling far too much to be convincingly upset about her girlfriend's antics. She flicked on her turn signal and merged over into the far right lane, taking the first exit they came upon. "I guess we're doing this the hard way."

By some horribly cruel twist of fate, or possibly good depending on your perspective on the situation, Cassidy had picked the perfect moment to start throwing a fit. As it so happened, the particular stretch of highway they'd been driving along was positively littered with tiny rest stops spread out

every few miles all up and down its feeder roads. All competing fiercely with one another to entice the motorists passing
them by to pull off for a quick break, to make use of their
restrooms, maybe enjoy a roadside picnic, or just resupply on
snacks and drinks from their little stores before continuing on
their way.

Not five minutes later, far, *far* sooner than Cassidy would
have liked, they were pulling up in front of a squat collection
of brick buildings arranged in a neat row in front of a modest
parking lot, with a small field and a handful of wooden picnic tables off to one side. Putting their car into park, Lauren
twisted in her seat and snatched her backpack from the seat
behind her. She took her time unzipping it with her usual
unhurried grace, and smiling broadly drew out the Attitude
Adjuster paddle from its tightly packed confines, giving it a
menacing whack against her palm once it was freed.

"Eep!"

The color had drained from Cassidy's face, as her eyes
stared transfixed at the bold white letters that spelled out her
impending doom.

"Come on then, cutie pie," said Lauren, pushing her door
open and standing to stretch her stiff limbs before leaning
back inside to pin her girlfriend in place with a predatory grin.
"We haven't got all day you know."

"Babe, I'm sorry," moaned Cassidy, even as her hands
started fumbling with her seatbelt and the handle on her door.
"Please just give me another chance. I *swear* I'll be good."

"No can do, hon," crooned Lauren, enjoying every moment
of the other girl's bubbling humiliation as she tiptoed tentatively around the back of their car to stand in front of her.
"You had your chance, and you blew it. Now it's time to pay

up."

"But-!"

The two of them made quite the sight as Lauren led the way through the parking lot, gripping the Attitude Adjuster by its handle in one hand, and her girlfriend's wrist in the other.

"Wait, hold on! Can't we talk about this, please?" whined Cassidy, anxiously trying to backpedal as she was dragged past the out buildings and toward the picnic tables just a few yards away from the women's restroom. She could see people milling about just outside its entrance, either waiting for a free stall to open up, or just killing time while someone they knew was in there, and the reality of what she'd gotten herself into was starting to crash down around her. With each step she could feel her face flushing a little bit hotter, as butterflies dive-bombed around inside her stomach.

"I *warned* you what was going to happen if you kept acting up," lectured Lauren, raising her voice enough so that the people they were passing by could get a good earful. "I made it very clear that if you couldn't behave yourself while we were driving, then I was going to pull over and put you across my knee. Didn't I, Cassie?"

"Yes, but," squeaked Cassidy, throwing a mortified look back over her shoulder at the small knot of people who had turned to watch them now. None of them could have mistaken her and Lauren as anything other than two lovers having a roadside spat, and while it was painfully obvious to everyone involved what was about to happen, they all just stayed where they were and looked on with amused indifference, preparing to enjoy the show.

"No buts," snapped Lauren, coming to a sudden stop at the first unoccupied picnic table she could find and putting her left foot up on its attached wooden bench. "Except *your* butt over my knee, now, missy."

She gave Cassidy's wrist an insistent pull, and the protesting girl toppled easily over her propped up thigh, landing with an adorable little "oomph!"

"Lauren, please, I promise I'll be good," moaned Cassidy, deciding to play her part to the fullest as she flailed her jack-knifed arms and legs ineffectually above the dirt, giving the people watching them just a handful of yards away something to snicker at as she glared at them petulantly.

"You'd damn well better be, cutie pie," growled Lauren playfully as she transferred the Attitude Adjuster to her left hand, freeing her right one up so that she could yank the loose fitting pair of denim cutoffs her girlfriend was wearing down to her knees, exposing the snug, forest-green bikini panties hidden underneath to any and all onlookers.

She let the temperature in Cassidy's cheeks rise by leaps and bounds for a few agonizingly long seconds as she lovingly rubbed her palm over her buns, before suddenly tugging her panties down to join her shorts, fully baring her pristinely white cheeks to the warm caress of the summer sun high above. Cassidy's squirming immediately went into overdrive at this, but before she could wrap her lips around any sort of coherent protest, her words were driven out of her in a squeal of pain.

SMACK!

The Attitude Adjuster collided with the centers of both cheeks at the same time, compressing them for a split-second before they sprang back into place with a mesmerizing wobble, now sporting a wide pink rectangle that marked the impact they'd just endured.

"Ow, hey!"

SMACK! SMACK!

Lauren smacked her again before she could say anything else, two swats back-to-back right across her sit-spots.

"Owie! Owie! Geez, watch it!"

"That's funny," observed Lauren, dryly arching an eyebrow as she stared down at her girlfriend's naked and only slightly-pink caboose. "I still haven't heard an apology yet."

"I'm sorry, I'm sorry, I'm sorry!" frantically squeaked out Cassidy in between yelps of pain as three extra-hard swats exploded against the lower half of her bottom.

"That's more like it," an amused Lauren snapped, pausing to rub the silky smooth wood of her paddle across Cassidy's sizzling seat. "Now let's just see if you can make me believe that."

It took another twenty fist-clenching, leg-flailing, cheek-scorching swats from the Attitude Adjuster before Lauren was finally convinced that her girlfriend's attitude had been sufficiently adjusted, and by then Cassidy's bottom was looking like it had caught one heck of a sunburn. It felt just about as hot as one too as she set her back on her feet, shorts and panties now tangled up around her ankles, and spent a few minutes straightening her hair back into place and delivering an off the cuff lecture about being obedient, before she pulled her in for a tight hug and a kiss.

"Do you need to go potty?" asked Lauren with a teasing smirk as she squatted down in front of the other girl and deftly straightened out her panties and shorts, pulling each back into place with over-exaggerated concern for Cassidy's throbbing cheeks. "Or maybe you'd like an ice pack from the store?"

"Hah, hah, very funny," pouted Cassidy, bobbing her fists impatiently at her sides and blushing almost as hot as her bottom felt as she tried not to pay attention to the handful of bemused people dispersing from their front row seats to her humiliation in front of the restrooms. "But no, I'm good, let's just get out of here."

"Sure thing, cutie pie," agreed Lauren, threading her right arm through Cassidy's left and leading the way back to their car, casually swinging the Attitude Adjuster in her free hand as they walked.

They were soon on their way again, and as Lauren pulled back out into traffic, she said, "Hey, do me a favor and call your mom for me real quick, will you?"

"Uh, okay..." answered Cassidy with a shrug, slipping her phone from her pocket and dialing her mother with a tap on her name from her speed dial. As it started to ring, Lauren plucked the device from her fingers, and put it on speaker. "Hey!"

"Shhh," hissed Lauren, and a moment later the call was answered.

"Hello?" came a friendly feminine voice from the other end of the line.

"Hi Misses Coleman, it's Lauren."

"Oh hello, dear, is everything alright?"

"Yeah, we're fine," she answered with a smirk, moving the phone out of Cassidy's reach before she could grab it. "Cassidy's here too, but she's kinda in the middle of getting something from the back seat while we're driving."

"Hi Mom," called Cassidy with a wave, flashing her

girlfriend a confused look at the lie as she flopped back into her seat, resigning herself to letting Lauren play out her little game.

"Hi honey, we're all so excited to see you!" answered Cassidy's mom.

"Us too," said Lauren. "But it looks like we're probably going to be a little later than we thought. The traffic's really starting to get bad, and we're stuck behind some construction right now."

"Hah, typical highways in the summer," sighed the older woman ruefully. "How much longer do you think you're going to be?"

"Oh, it shouldn't be much more than an hour, I'd say," shrugged Lauren. "Forty-five minutes if we're lucky."

"Well, that's not too bad," Cassidy's mother observed. "That'll still give us plenty of time to make our reservations."

"Excellent," answered Lauren, sounding relieved. "We'll see you soon then."

"Alright then, drive safe. Bye Cassidy, bye Lauren. Love you!"

"Bye Mom, love you too," called Cassidy, accepting her phone back and hanging up.

"What was that all about?" she asked a moment later, scooting forward in her seat to get a better look out the windshield and further down the road. "There's not any serious traffic right now..."

"No," agreed Lauren, smiling wolfishly and moving to pass another car. "But there *are* about four more of those rest stops between here and your parents' house, and you and I are going to be stopping at each and every one of them to have a little chat about your attitude."

"Eep!"

Chapter 9

Birthday Bashed Buns

Cassidy's birthday party the following evening ended up being a rather intimate family affair due largely to the fact that all of her friends from the local community college and her short stint as an usher at the movie theater down the street from her parent's house had either moved away, or were out of town on family vacations of their own. As a result, the guest list for that night consisted of just her mother and father, Lauren, and Melody, her eighteen year old little sister who had just graduated from high school only a few weeks earlier. Cassidy didn't really mind this all that much though, she much preferred cozy family gatherings to big blowout bashes anyway. Plus, a smaller party would mean more money for presents, right?

The celebration itself wound up being not all that different from a regular Sunday dinner at the Coleman house, but it was still nevertheless a good time. Cassidy's mother had hung up a bunch of multicolored streamers all over the place and a glittery banner above the kitchen table that read "Happy Birthday Cassidy" in big bright letters to help set the mood, her father had grilled up the juiciest steaks the grocery store had to offer, and come seven o'clock that evening they all sat down to share a wonderful meal together of mouth-watering steak, steamed vegetables, and homemade garlic mashed potatoes. None of the food was particularly fancy, but it was all delicious, and dinner ended up lasting for quite a while as the family got to know Lauren a little bit better.

As luck would have it, Lauren had actually hit it off quite well with Cassidy's parents and her little sister almost immediately upon arriving. Her natural charisma and understated athletic grace had easily won them all over, and by the time they'd sat down for dinner at the Italian restaurant her father had made reservations for them at, it was like she was a part of the family. And while this was a major relief for Cassidy to be sure, it was also proving to be a bit of an embarrassing nuisance as well. Her mother had taken a real shine to Lauren as she'd gotten to know her over their fancy food the night before, and it hadn't taken either of them long to realize that they both shared a mutual love of gently teasing Cassidy and calling her out on her attitude whenever she was being a brat; much to her dismay. The two of them had even somehow managed to perfect their simultaneous disapproving scowls by the time dessert was served, and poor Cassidy had been stuck having to deal with the two of them having a ball ganging up on her off and on ever since.

In fact, if she hadn't known any better, she would have *sworn* that she'd come within a hair's breadth of being dragged off to an out of the way family restroom by one or both of them for a quick spanking on more than one occasion that afternoon while they'd been out shopping at the mall. Cassidy was fairly sure that if it had just been her and Lauren alone that afternoon, then she definitely would have spent at least some of their outing with a sore bottom, but thankfully her girlfriend kept her urge to embarrass her in check enough so that the topic of spanking never actually came up. At least, she hoped it hadn't. It was sometimes hard to tell what her girlfriend and her mother were talking about when they walked ahead of her and murmured quietly to each other. More than a few times Cassidy had found herself lagging behind and complaining about having to be dragged to seemingly *every* store in the mall so the two of them could play dress-up with her, and as a result she'd missed a decent amount of their chit-chatting, but one thing that she hadn't missed was the way one or both of them would look back at her with an arched eyebrow, staring at her with an unimpressed coolness until her whining suddenly dried up.

Well, truth be told, Cassidy didn't mind the whole dress-up thing all *that* much. Sure it was a little embarrassing to be pinched and prodded as she turned in slow circles to show off whatever clothes the two of them had picked out for her, but they at least respected her wishes and let her use each store's dressing room alone, at least after she whined enough about them seeing her in her underwear long enough. Lauren had a great eye for outfits that flattered her natural curves and made her feel very pretty, and her mother seemed to agree. That last part in particular was a major relief, because while Lauren may have been picking the outfits, it was Misses Coleman who was the one bankrolling their entire operation. So it was that Cassidy found herself coming home that afternoon laden down with several new outfits that she just couldn't wait to mix into her daily rotation, and that Lauren couldn't wait to strip off of her at the first opportunity.

After dinner was finished and they'd ran out of steam reminiscing about Cassidy's life as an angsty teenager and all the things Melody had been up to since she'd last seen her over Christmas break, it was time to move on to cake and presents. Cassidy had definitely been looking forward to this all throughout their meal, due in no small part to the fact that she'd gotten a sneak peek at some of the things her mother had rung up that afternoon when she thought she hadn't been looking. Since she was the birthday girl, she got to stay seated with Lauren while her parents and sister cleared away the dishes from the table, and a few minutes later her mother and father had laid out a magnificent looking cookie-crumble birthday cake before her, along with some paper plates and plastic silverware. Candles soon followed, and once they'd been lit and the appropriate number of pictures had been taken with Cassidy beaming over her cake alongside Lauren, her sister, both of her parents, and then all of them together, they all sang Happy Birthday to her and she blew the tiny flames out with one long breath.

"So, cake or presents first?" asked Mister Coleman, sliding the heavy slab of sprinkles and frosting over to his end of the table where he began to cut it up into more manageable square pieces.

"Presents, presents!" cheered Cassidy. "Cake can wait. I'm absolutely *dying* to see what you and mom have been hiding from me all afternoon."

"Works for me," nodded Lauren, just as eager to watch her girlfriend unwrap her gifts as she was to do the unwrapping. She knew she was going to love them.

"What, no birthday spanking?" protested Melody, trying to sound indignant, but doing nothing to hide the playful grin on her face. "You kept insisting that *I* get one before I could open any of *my* presents last year you know."

"Yeah, but I'm older, so I don't have to," dismissed Cassidy with a laugh, leaning over and snatching up one of the smaller presents from the other end of the table where her mother had piled them up.

"That's not fair," whined Melody. "If I had to get one, then so should you!"

That just made Cassidy stick her tongue out at her, clearly reveling in being the older sibling.

"Mom!"

"You know," interrupted Lauren, sliding smoothly into the conversation between the two of them before they could devolve into full-on sibling bickering. "She *does* have a point, Cassie."

"No she doesn't!" squeaked Cassidy, going pink in the face as everyone around the table smirked at her.

"Birthday spanking, birthday spanking, birthday spanking!" Melody started to chant from her seat across from her, her parents soon joining in a few moments later, laughing.

"Uh-oh, it sounds like the people have spoken," declared Lauren, turning to rap a finger against the tip of her girlfriend's nose with a wink. "Sorry, birthday girl, but it looks like older sisters aren't immune from getting their birthday spankings after all."

"But I thought you said I got to be queen for a day?" huffed Cassidy good-naturedly, accepting her defeat, but refusing to do so without at least some semblance of a fight. "As queen, I hereby outlaw this tradition!"

"Well then, consider this a revolution, your majesty," teased Lauren as she slid her chair back a couple of feet from the edge of the table and patted her lap. "I assume none of you mind if I do the honors? She *is* my girlfriend after all."

"Of course not," dismissed Cassidy's father with a negligent, setting aside his frosting-strewn cake knife and grinning.

"Go for it, hon," agreed her mother, making a point of plucking the present Cassidy had picked out from her hands and returning it to the pile. "You can have this *after* you've had your birthday spanking, young lady."

"You're all traitors to the crown," grumbled Cassidy, pouting theatrically and glaring at the table in front of her as she slid her own chair back and moved to stand by Lauren's side with a defiant swish of her hips.

"Love you too, cutie pie," laughed Lauren, taking her by the wrist with her left hand, and placing her right palm along the small of her back, rubbing it for a moment before guiding her down into position across her lap.

"Harrumph!"

"Oooh, I see London, I see France," jeered Melody, standing up and leaning forward with her palms on the table, angling for the best possible vantage point for the upcoming festivities. "I see Cassidy's underpants!"

"You wha-?"

That certainly got Cassidy's tush squirming, though it did very little to help hide the lower-third of her panties that had inadvertently peeked out from underneath the hem of her brand new dress as she'd bent over her girlfriend's lap.

"Lauren," she moaned, elongating the word into a prolonged whine as she flailed her fists impotently against the other girl's left calf. "Do something!"

"Whatever you say, hon," Lauren answered cheerfully, feeling mischief coil and spring within her as she oh so casually twitched the back of her girlfriend's dress up past her hips, fully exposing the rainbow-maned unicorns galloping whimsically across the snugly-contoured seat of her arctic-blue cheeky briefs.

"Eep!" squeaked Cassidy, her heart leaping into her throat as her legs scissored frantically behind her.

"Aaaw, Cassidy Anne, those are just *adorable*," cooed her mother, rising halfway out of her chair next to her husband to get a better angle for a quick snapshot with her phone.

"They certainly are," agreed Lauren, giving the unicorns a friendly pat. "You weren't trying to show off for your birthday spanking by wearing something so cute, *were* you?"

"Oh my god, you guys are the literal fucking worst right now," grumbled a mortified and cherry-faced Cassidy. Her cheeks were so hot just then, that she was half-afraid that her face was about to melt off onto the floor. Still though, she couldn't help but smile in chagrin and laugh along with the rest of them at the predicament she found herself in. "Owie! Hey!"

"Language, missy," warned Lauren with a half-smirk, having just delivered a sharp swat to the center of her seat for her potty mouth. She casually let her right hand slide over a couple of inches, just barely hooking her thumb into the elastic of Cassidy's waistband right where the top slopes of her two cheeks met. "Do you *really* think you should be pushing your luck right now?"

"Yeah, Cassidy," sneered Melody. "Watch your mouth."

"Just because it's your birthday doesn't mean I can't find a bar of soap for you to suck on while you're getting spanked, young lady," added her mother darkly. "Three's still three more boxes of Ivory waiting under the sink from last time."

"Whatever," snorted Cassidy, getting the message loud and clear and wondering fretfully if Lauren would really be so bold as to bare her bottom in front of her family like she seemed to be threatening to. "You guys can't get mad at me. I'm still the birthday girl here, and the birthday girl gets to say whatever she wants. That's the rules."

"Are you sure about that one, sweetie?" asked her father with a snort of his own.

"Well then, *birthday girl*, here's a birthday spanking for your birthday butt," declared Lauren with a laugh, gripping Cassidy tight around the waist with her left hand, and raising her right palm up high over her shoulder with a dramatic flourish. "Ready everyone?"

"Ready!"

SLAP!

"One!" they all cried together.

SLAP!

"Two!" they echoed.

Though the entire ordeal was certainly humiliating, thankfully the spanks themselves were little more than hard pats, and by the end of it Cassidy's tush only carried a mildly-warm tingle as everyone finally shouted out.

"And one to grow on!"

Cassidy didn't need a mirror to know that her face was a lot pinker than her bottom was just then, but she had to admit that it had been rather fun having Lauren give her a birthday spanking at her own party, even if it *had* been with the back of her dress rucked up over hips. Luckily, the entire ordeal had only lasted maybe five minutes, and now that it was finally over she could right herself and fix her clothes and go back to pretending that her sister and parents hadn't just watched her get spanked at the dinner table. Plus there was still that pile of presents calling her name to attend to, and as far she was concerned, she'd *definitely* earned them by now.

"Hold her still for just a sec, Lauren. I want to get a picture of you two together like that before either of you gets up," ordered Cassidy's mother, rising from her chair and slowly circling around the two of them in search of the best angle.

"Sure, no problem," agreed Lauren with a laugh, pinning her birthday girlfriend in place with her left arm and grinning from ear to ear as the shutter sound on Misses Coleman's camera app clicked away. "Say cheese, cutie pie."

"Cheese, cutie pie," grumbled Cassidy, pursing her lips into a defiant pout.

SMACK!

"Ow, hey!"

"You need to smile," teased Lauren, rubbing her palm across the spot where she'd just cracked her palm in a proper spank. "Right, Malory?"

"That's right, dear," agreed Cassidy's mother with a matching smirk. "There you go, much better."

And so it was that Cassidy's first birthday party with her girlfriend became one of the most memorable celebrations of her young life, and unfortunately also kicked off a humiliating new tradition for their family birthday gatherings. She just hoped that none of them would overhear Lauren dishing out her *real* birthday spanking later that night. She'd promised her before dinner that she'd be giving her one, and somehow she had a feeling her girlfriend would be determined that she start the next year of her life off with a *very* well-adjusted attitude.

Chapter 10

Sunday Scuffles and Switched Sisters

"Oh my fucking god," squealed Melody, jumping to her feet and hurling a pillow at her older sister. "You are *such* a bitch!"

"Oh what-fucking-ever," snapped Cassidy, springing up just as quickly to face her sister, her nostrils flaring. "You can watch your stupid show anytime you want online anyway, so who cares if you don't get to watch it now?"

The fight had been brewing ever since they'd all gone out for brunch that Sunday morning the day after Cassidy's birthday party. It had started small enough, with the two of them arguing over who got to sit in the front seat of their father's SUV (It had just been easier to just pile into the one oversized car rather than take two of them), and had been steadily escalating ever since. Now the tension between the two sisters had reached a boiling point as they stood mere inches away from each another, hurling accusations and insults with steadily increasing volume and ferocity.

"Uh… Cassie, honey, it really isn't that big of a deal you know," Lauren tried to intercede gently, but firmly. She stepped in closer and put a warning hand on her girlfriend's shoulder, hoping that would be enough to snap her out of it. "Why don't we just watch what Melody wants to, okay? She *did* call dibs on the TV, after all."

Her attempts to interject a bit of calmness between the two

of them went totally ignored however, and a moment later things finally snapped. One of them pushed the other, in the confusion it was impossible to tell for certain who actually started it, and the next thing Lauren knew, the two sisters were rolling around on the floor wrestling like kids half their age. As an only child, Lauren had never experienced first-hand what quarrelling with a younger sister was like, and as such found herself standing over the two of them dumbstruck as they grappled and cursed, trying unsuccessfully to get their attention and cool their raging tempers. Thankfully, a more experienced sibling wrangler swooped in just then, and she was able to step back and let her handle it.

"Cassidy Anne! Melody Jane! You two stop fighting this instant!" bellowed their mother, storming into the living room and descending upon the two of them like a hurricane as she pulled them apart from each other with practiced ease.

"She started it!" they both exclaimed at the same time, each pointing an accusatory finger at the other and glaring.

"Are you two *serious*?" demanded their mother in exasperation, letting go of the backs of their shirts and throwing her hands into the air, before looking over to Lauren as if she could somehow make things better. "You both are way, *way*, too old to be acting like this. I can't believe it. What are you, five?"

She sighed loudly and pinched the bridge of her nose between her thumb and forefinger.

"I'm sorry you had to see that, Lauren dear," she said, moving to stand beside her so they could both scowl disapprovingly at the two sisters who now stood side by side shamefacedly staring at their bare feet. "These two can be *such* brats when they get around each other. I swear it's like they're half their age sometimes."

"Yes, I think I see what you mean," laughed Lauren, hoping to lift the heavy mood just a little bit now that the hostilities had been so effectively doused.

"You have no idea how much part of me wishes that they were both still young enough to go over my knee for fighting like that," lamented Malory Coleman as she ran a hand over her forehead and through her curly hair. 'You'd be amazed how quickly the hatchet got buried whenever Mommy said it was time for a spanking."

That made Cassidy and her sister both blush and squirm uncomfortably, neither of them daring to speak up just then as memories of double-spankings from their childhood and early teens started replaying in their minds. Noticing the effect their mother's words was having on them, Lauren sensed the beginnings of an idea starting to take root, and she struck.

"You know," she started to say, drawing the words out contemplatively as she fixed the two sisters in front of her with an unimpressed frown. "After what I've just seen, I don't know if it's really all that accurate to say that they *are* too old for a little bit of sibling spanking. They were certainly acting the part just now, and if you ask me, I think a little reminder of what happens when you misbehave would do them both a world of good."

"No it wouldn't!" Cassidy hastened to reassure the two frowning women standing in front of her.

"Yeah, Mom, we're sorry we screwed up," added Melody, frantically nodding her agreement beside her siser. "But let's not get ahead of ourselves."

"Hmmm..." mused Misses Coleman, rubbing her chin thoughtfully as she gradually started to warm to Lauren's suggestion. "I think you might have a point, dear. As much as I hate to admit it, the two of them have definitely been acting a lot more like a pair of spoiled middle schoolers than actual adults pretty much all day. I mean honestly, rolling around on the floor and pulling each other's hair? That's just ridiculous."

"Very," agreed Lauren, smugly crossing her arms under her chest and shaking her head.

"Mooom," whined Cassidy and Melody together.

"Whaaat?" replied their mother, matching her daughters' over exaggerated melodrama with her own voice as she rolled her eyes.

"It was her fault!" they both declared, each pointing a finger at the other and glowering again. Neither one was willing to admit any fault just then, especially with a spanking possibly on the line now. It was hard to tell if their mother was being serious about Lauren's suggestion or not, but neither of them wanted to take any chances if they could avoid it.

"I don't care *who* started it, girls," snapped Misses Coleman, making up her mind right there and then as she planted her hands firmly on her hips and leaned forward to loom over her two petulant daughters. "It takes two to tango, and as far as I'm concerned you're both guilty, and you're *both* going to get one heck of a whoopin' for the way you've been acting today."

"But that's not fair," moaned Cassidy, going pale alongside her sister and actually stomping her foot with the injustice of it all.

"Please, Mom, we're sorry!" Melody hurriedly added, her hands having come together in front of her, begging.

"It's way too late to say you're sorry now, girls," snapped

their mother, holding a palm out to forestall any more pro-tests. "The two of you have had this coming for a while now, and you've got nobody to blame but yourselves for what's about to happen."

She let the two of them stew in their shame and worry for a few long moments, each of them pink-faced and fiddling nervously with the hem of their shirt as they tried to look any-where but at their mother or Lauren. Then, once the gravity of their situation had more or less fully sunk in, Misses Coleman cleared her throat and got down to business.

"Alright girls, you know the drill," she said, her tone now brusque and business-like as she clapped her hands twice in quick succession. "I want those pants off, and the two of you out cutting me some switches, *now*. It may have been a while since we've had to do this, but you still know the kind I'm looking for, so don't try and get away with anything weak and floppy. I want two good ones from each of you. The scissors are still in the drawer by the fridge, so get hopping, unless you'd like me to make it *three* switches instead."

She turned her back on the two of them then, and waved a negligent hand over her shoulder in dismissal as she moved to pick up the sofa cushions that had been knocked to the ground in her daughters' earlier brawl.

"Lauren and I will be out to deal with you in *ten* minutes, and we'd better find you both with your noses glued to that wall on the back porch when we do. Is that clear?"

"Uh , Malory..." ventured Lauren hesitantly. On the one hand she was elated that her prodding had produced such exciting results, but on the other she was starting to worry that she might have bitten off just a little bit more than she could chew. "Are you sure you want me tagging along?"

"Of course, dear," the older woman reassured her, straightening two more pillows and flashing her an encouraging smile. "Switching a bratty butt couldn't be easier, and having you there to take care of Cassidy will save me the extra effort of having to tan two hides back to back."

"Oh my god, Mom, are you serious?" whined Cassidy, her face growing noticeably pinker than her younger sister's as she heard this.

"Yes I *am* serious," snapped Misses Coleman, whirling around to face her daughter and leveling a sharp glare at her. "And the two of you had better have your pants off and your butts in gear by the time I count to three, or else Lauren is going to get see how we handle bedtime spankings in this house as well. Now scoot!"

"Eep!" the two sisters squeaked in unison, their hands immediately flying to the clasps on their pants as their mother began a slow count on her fingers.

By the time she'd reached "two and a half", they'd both shoved their tight-fitting jeans down to their ankles, skewing their panties halfway along their thighs in the process. With much hopping about and kicking, they were eventually able to free their feet from their stylish, but snug, confines and were frantically scampering out of the room and toward the kitchen while trying to cover their half-exposed cheeks as their mother slowly dragged out the word "three".

"Those two," sighed Misses Coleman with a wistful smile tugging at the corners of her lips once she and Lauren were alone together in the living room. Stooping down to pick up Melody's black jeggings from where she'd kicked them off beside the TV, she folded them neatly and set them on the arm of the sofa as Lauren did the same with Cassidy's own discarded skinny jeans. The two of them then took a seat to share a quiet conversation about what was going to happen in the next few minutes, Misses Coleman filling Lauren in on the exact procedure for how she handled switching her daughters whenever they were disobedient enough to need it.

Twenty minutes later, they'd decided to wait a bit longer to give the two girls time to properly clean their switches and let their imaginations run wild with ideas about how they would feel being used on them, Lauren and Misses Coleman stepped out onto the wraparound back porch of the house. There they found Cassidy and Melody standing side by side, waiting for their punishment just as they had every other time they'd been sent out back to wait for a switching together. They had the tips of their noses pressed against the dark-gray siding wall beside the back door, their fingers were interlaced on top of their heads, and their feet were spaced out about a shoulder's width apart.

While definitely being uncomfortable, the position of their arms around their heads also had the added benefit of raising the hems of their shirts up well past their waists, fully exposing the panties clinging to their soon to be striped bottoms hiding just beneath. Lauren had to admit to herself as she shifted her gaze back and forth from Cassidy's black and white lace briefs, and her younger sister's more daring maroon thong, that they both had been dealt a very good genetic hand when it came to well-padded rear ends. A fact that they would both probably be grateful for in a few minutes when said rear ends started collecting welts.

"Alright you two, let's see how well you followed my instructions," declared their mother as she moved to where the four supple switches and the pair of kitchen scissors had been left for her on the seat of one of the patio chairs. Lauren joined her, and together they ran their fingers along the pruned lengths of thin and whippy, still very green and bendy branches, feeling the small bumps here and there where off-shoot growths had been trimmed away.

THWIP! THWIP!

They gave each neatly trimmed branch a few test swishes through the air, and then nodded, satisfied.

"I'm happy to see that even though it's been a while, you both still know how to cut a proper switch," said Misses Coleman with grim amusement. "Hopefully this will be the last time either of you ever has to put those skills to use."

"Yes ma'am," mumbled the two sullen girls awaiting their punishment, neither of them daring to turn away from their spot facing the wall of the house.

"Now normally I line the two of them up side by side over the railing here and take turns walloping them," Misses Coleman went on to explain to Lauren, more for Cassidy and Melody's benefit since she'd already gone over this with her earlier when they'd been waiting for the two of them to finish getting their switches ready. "But since you're here, we can knock them both out at the same time without any breaks."

"Sounds good to me," agreed Lauren with a broad smirk, swishing each of her two switches through the air beside her, trying to decide which she was going to use first. Settling on one, she flicked it sharply against the back of her girlfriend's unprotected left thigh. "Get your butt over the railing right now, cutie pie."

"Ah!" hissed Cassidy through clenched teeth, her left hand flying down to where she'd just been swatted as she slowly turned around to pout at Lauren. Lauren just met her glower with an implacable grin and a wink however, and she knew she'd lost. And so, heaving a long sigh, Cassidy made the short trip of a few steps across the porch and over to the white-painted wooden railing that ran around the entire perimeter of her parents' house and leaned forward to rest her elbows on it.

"*All* the way over, Cassidy Anne," admonished her mother, encouraging her to obey with another quick flick of a switch to the back of her right thigh this time. "Get that caboose nice and high for Lauren."

"Ack! Geez, okay, okay!" she squawked in protest, all but throwing herself across the sturdy top crossbar at her waist and bending so far forward that she wound up standing on her tip-toes and gripping two of the vertical posts in front of her for support.

"That's, *better*," huffed Misses Coleman, before directing her full attention to her other daughter who'd turned from her spot against the wall at some point and had been watching the proceedings with a self-satisfied smirk. "You too, Melody Jane. Get that butt bent over, and fast. We haven't got all day, you know. I've still got to get dinner started."

"Yes ma'am," piped up Melody, fleeing from the wall in a hurry and finding a spot a few feet down the railing from her sister to bend over.

"Oh my god, they're just so *cute*," snickered Lauren low enough under her breath so that only Misses Coleman would be able to hear her. "How can you stand it?"

"With lots of love and attention," answered the other woman wryly, giving one of her switches a meaningful swish beside her.

They spent a few more moments savoring the spectacle of

the squirming seats before them, before Lauren broke the spell with a question.

"Panties down?"

"Panties *off*," corrected Misses Coleman with a grim nod. "They won't be needing them for a while, trust me."

"Works for me," cooed Lauren as she sashayed her way over to her girlfriend and slipped the fingers of both hands into the lace-trimmed waistband of her panties. She tugged them down to her ankles in one smooth motion, and then slipped them free of first one bare foot and then the other while her mother did the same with Melody.

"I'm not really sure I like you wearing things like this all that much, Melody dear," clucked Misses Coleman disapprovingly as she snatched up her daughter's thong from the porch, prompting an unseen eye roll from the other girl as she examined the insubstantial bit of fabric critically.

"I'll be taking these," Lauren cooed smugly at the same time, straightening up from her crouch behind Cassidy and tucking her girlfriend's still-warm panties into her back pocket, patting them fondly. She was already looking forward to all the ways she was going to make her earn them back later that night as she lined up her chosen switch along the centers of Cassidy's cheeks and gave them a few experimental taps.

"Remember, it's all in the wrist, dear," advised Misses Coleman as she likewise took aim against Melody's clenching and unclenching bare bottom. "Flick it, don't smack it, and be sure to keep things nice and speedy. I want them dancing and hollering up a storm, not trying to grit their teeth and ride it out in silence."

"Right," said Lauren with a nod of her head, readjusting

her grip on the switch in her hand and immediately noticing an improvement in the way it felt as she snapped it through the air in slow motion against Cassidy's rump. "How many?"

"Oh honey," laughed the older woman as if she'd just been asked if the tooth fairy were real. "This is a *switching*, not a paddling. You just keep flicking away until that stick in your hands starts to fall apart, and then move on to the next one. It's light enough that you're not going to hurt her, much, and she'll definitely be thinking twice about fighting once it's gone to pieces. Oh, and don't forget the thighs either, I want to see two well-welted little girls by the time we're finished here."

"Can do," answered Lauren, flashing her girlfriend's mother a sloppy half-salute with her switch before taking aim once again and letting it fly full-force.

THWIP! THWIP! THWIP! THWIP! THWIP!

Moving at a brisk and relentless pace, Lauren and Misses Coleman proceeded to switch the ever-loving daylights out of the two bent over sisters. Falling into a steady rhythm, they layered on a thick blanket of mostly-horizontal overlapping welts from just a few inches above their knees, to the very tops of their wriggling cheeks, swatting seemingly at random but never pausing until finally, mercifully, both switches had been worn out and were left as little more than green bits of splintered twigs littering the patio floor.

Cassidy and Melody were both left sobbing by the time it was all over, each of them having promised vehemently over and over again to never so much as even speak a harsh word to one another ever again. Each was covered in a fine sheen of sweat that made their off-white tops cling to their shoulders and upper backs where they'd ridden up to show off their pale lower abdomens, having grown semi-transparent with the moisture and now revealing the light-colored bras they were wearing underneath. They both stayed flopped over the railing, neither of them doing much more than panting and moaning piteously as each beat of their hearts sent a fresh pulse of pain through their throbbing flesh, highlighting each tender welt in exquisite detail and driving the aching pain deeper and deeper into them.

"Come here, you," cooed Lauren as she gently helped Cassidy back to her feet and wrapped her in a loving embrace, letting her cry against her shoulder for a minute or two while she fought to get herself back under control. Once her sobbing had subsided to just the occasional sniffle and hiccup, she released her and spent a few more moments fixing her hair and smiling gently into her red-rimmed eyes, while her mother did much the same with Melody Then, with a firm grip on her upper arm, she marched her back to her spot facing the wall beside the back door, and arranged her hands once again on top of her head while Melody and her mother did likewise.

"You two can stay just like that until I call you in for dinner," declared Misses Coleman, much of the earlier steel now gone from her voice, but still sounding like she wouldn't hesitate to make them cut another switch if they sassed her. "No moving, no talking, and definitely no rubbing. Is that understood?"

"Yes ma'am," came the twin watery echoes from in front of them.

"Good, because if I have to come back out here…" she let the warning go unfinished, but still punctuated it with a sharp slap to all four of the battered buns arranged before her.

"Ack! Ow!"

"Owie! Oh!"

Their mother straightened up and smirked, more than a little satisfied with the reactions she'd just wrung out of her daughters.

"Come along, Lauren dear. Let's leave these two to their timeout."

—

"Phew," sighed Misses Coleman a few minutes later as she poured herself a cup of coffee and one for Lauren. "I always forget how much of a workout it is to spank those two. Thanks for your help back there, hon."

"No problem," replied Lauren, accepting the warm mug with a lopsided grin and flexing her own tired wrist. "I was happy to help."

"I'm sure you were," laughed the older woman, smilingly knowingly at her over the top of her mug as she took a sip. "But seriously, dear, I'm so glad that you and Cassidy found each other. I've never seen her so happy."

"Well…" Misses Coleman paused and set her mug down with a smirk, nodding her head in the direction of the back door they'd left propped open just a few inches and the two still-sniffling girls standing just out of sight beside it. "You know what I mean."

"I do," confirmed Lauren with a twinkle in her eye. "Even when she's being a total brat, I wouldn't trade my time with Cassie for anything in the world."

"Awww, you two are just so sweet together," gushed Misses Coleman, wiping away a tear from the corner of her eye. "Cassidy is such a wonderful girl, and I couldn't be happier that she's managed to find such wonderful girlfriend. Her father and I love seeing you two together. You really do bring out a special light in each other that's just so wonderful to see."

"Oh, well uh…" stammered Lauren, lost for words and feeling her face heating up to match the mug she suddenly found herself fidgeting with. "Th-thank you."

"Of course, dear," answered Misses Coleman, reaching out and patting the back of Lauren's left hand in a motherly fashion. Her lips then twitched up into a smirk and she added. "And if she *ever* gives you any attitude in the future, I want you to feel free to put her right over your knee. Lord knows she could use it."

"Hah," snorted Lauren, smirking right back at the older woman and giving her a conspiratorial wink. "I'm *sure* that won't be necessary."

Epilogue

— *ONE YEAR LATER* —

Cassidy Anne Coleman, soon to be Misses Cassidy Anne Delaney, stood in front of the ornate full-length mirror that dominated one side of the little room she'd been stashed away in while she waited for the ceremony to begin. Not that she minded. She couldn't stop beaming at herself in her reflection as she made a few final adjustments here and there to her hair and wedding dress. Today was the big day. It was finally happening!

"You look great, Cass," said Melody from beside her, flashing her older sister a thumbs up in the mirror.

"Thanks," squeaked Cassidy, positively bubbling with pent up excitement.

"Knock, knock," called a familiar voice from the other side of the door to the room, not bothering to wait for an invitation to come in as the person it belonged to pushed it open and stepped inside.

"Oh wow, Cassie, you look *spectacular*," cooed Lauren, pausing in the doorway to look her bride-to-be up and down with a long, low whistle.

"I know, right?" demanded Melody, moving to stand beside her future sister-in-law so they could both goggle at her.

"Isn't it supposed to be bad luck for you to see the bride before the wedding?" teased Cassidy, blushing at all the attention she was getting, but still beaming.

"I don't think that counts if we're both the bride," countered Lauren with a smirk, swishing her way over to her and planting a quick kiss on her cheek. "Can you give us a minute, Mel?"

"Sure thing," agreed Melody, slipping out of the room with a wave. "Don't take too long now you two, the ceremony is supposed to start in… ten minutes. You wouldn't want to be the first people in history to ever have a wedding start late, now would you?"

"We won't, we won't," reassured Lauren, waving the other girl off with a laugh.

"So," said Cassidy, an eager grin spreading across her blushing cheeks once the door had shut firmly behind her maid of honor. "Are you going to show me what you've been hiding behind your back or what?"

"Of course," purred Lauren, bringing her hands out from behind her and holding out a long, thin box to her future wife. It was made from stiff white cardboard, and had a glittering white ribbon tied in a bow around its middle. "I know it's a little early for wedding gifts, but I wanted you to have this one before the ceremony began."

"What is it?" asked Cassidy as she accepted the box and hefted it appraisingly. It was surprisingly heavy.

"Open it," Lauren encouraged her with a wink.

Her curiosity now piqued, Cassidy pulled the ribbon free and let it flutter to the floor, tossing the lid of the box after it a moment later.

"Oh wow!"

Inside, laid out artfully across a bed of tissue paper, was a leather strap. It looked to be about the same length as her

Attitude Adjuster paddle, maybe just a little bit longer, and was slightly wider than a regular belt, though it was nearly twice as thick as one she saw as she plucked it from the box and ran her fingers along its length. The leather was stiff and smelled richly of oil. Its edges were glassy smooth and had been stitched with a border of white thread that offset the black material of the strap beautifully. However her favorite part, the part that made her heart leap with fear and excitement into her throat, was the sweeping white letters embroidered along its length that spelled out the phrase "Delaney Family Discipline".

"Do... do you like it?" asked Lauren hesitantly, breaking into her thoughts and looking uncharacteristically nervous.

"I love it," sniffed Cassidy, her eyes growing misty as she threw her arms around Lauren and kissed her hard, not caring if it smudged her lipstick. "It's perfect!"

"Phew," laughed Lauren with a sigh of relief when she was finally able to come up for air some time later. "Now bend over."

THE END

More Books by Clarine Klein
(Available on Amazon)

Back to Her Teens

Clarine Klein

Back to Her Teens

Petite and oh so sassy college sophomore Rhen Mathews is being kicked out of her dorms to make room for new students, and is in desperate need of a place to live. And so, when Dana Johnson, her former boss from her brief stint as an assistant at a local daycare, offers to let her move in with her for free, she accepts without a second thought.

The only condition?

She has to do so as her thirteen-year-old niece from out of town.

What follows is a forced regression/ageplay novel filled to the brim with super embarrassing moments for Rhen and lots of much-needed spanking and discipline from her loving, but very strict, Auntie Dana.

The SPANKING of
Sally Marie

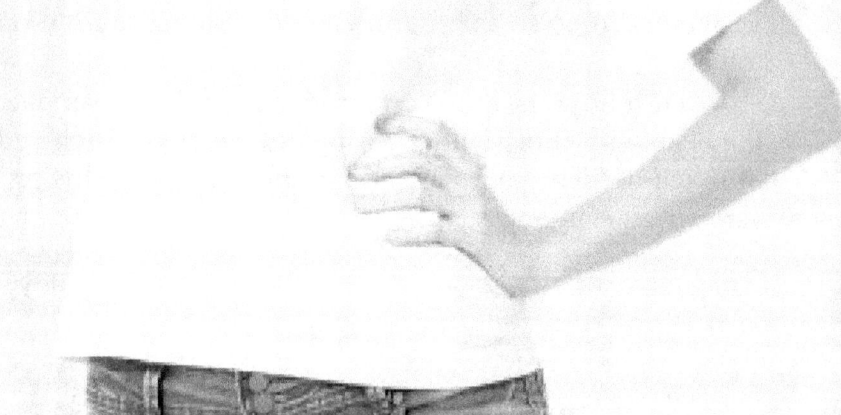

CLARINE KLEIN

The Spanking of Sally Marie

Sally finds herself in trouble once too often, and as grounding and other forms of punishment have had little effect on Sally's bratty behavior, her parents decide to spank their teenage daughter instead. It all begins when Sally stays up half the night playing around on her computer. Her dad is not pleased, and upends her for a bare bottom spanking. It is the first of many such spankings delivered by either Mom or Dad, and things get mega embarrassing for Sally when she's spanked in the Ladies Room in the mall, and in a side room at the local church during the Sunday service. Sally soon finds out the difference between 'attitude adjuster' spankings and the real thing, and her humiliation increases when her girlfriends find out she's still getting spanked - they even seize an opportunity to spank her themselves!

Thank you for reading!